MILLS & BOON

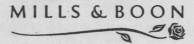

FAVOURITES

A chance to read and collect some of the best-loved novels
from Mills & Boon – the world's largest publisher of romantic
fiction.

Every month, two titles by favourite Mills & Boon authors
will be republished in the *Favourites* series.

DEDICATION

To all the women who have had or will
have breast cancer

A donation from the proceeds of this book
will be made to:
THE IMPERIAL CANCER RESEARCH FUND
44, LINCOLN'S INN FIELDS
LONDON WC2

Sally Wentworth

BROKEN
DESTINY

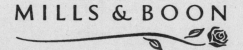

MILLS & BOON LIMITED
ETON HOUSE, 18-24 PARADISE ROAD
RICHMOND, SURREY TW9 1SR

*MILLS & BOON, the Rose Device
and Favourites are trademarks of the publisher.*

*First published in Great Britain 1990
by Mills & Boon Limited*

© Sally Wentworth 1990

*Australian copyright 1990
Philippine copyright 1991
This edition 1994*

ISBN 0 263 78946 2

*Set in Times Roman 10$^1/_2$ on 12pt.
02-9411-51771 C*

Printed and bound in Great Britain

CHAPTER ONE

As THEY emerged from the Tube station, Jancy glanced up and saw a barrage balloon floating in the sky, the evening sunlight reflecting off its silver skin like a huge oval mirror. 'Look.' She nudged Vicki and pointed. They paused for a moment, heads raised, then hurried on down the road to the sandbag-protected entrance of the dance-hall, where a white-helmeted MP was on duty.

'Evening, girls.' He gave their slim figures in the blue WRAF uniforms an approving once-over. 'Forces pay-box on the left.'

Pushing aside the blackout curtains, they bought their tickets and walked down a right-angled corridor and through a pair of double doors, to emerge into a whole new world of bright lights and music. It was a vast place, this *palais de dance*: over on the left was a wide, flag-decked stage on which a full-sized band of men in GI uniforms was playing the latest Glenn Miller tunes, there was a bar at the far end that stretched the whole width of the hall, and on the right another, much smaller stage where a well-known singer was busily signing autographs. But what struck them most of all was the number of people there. All the tables around the room were taken, the dance floor was crowded, and there was a mass of people standing at the sides.

The two girls stood for a moment near the entrance, taking in the scene. 'There are loads of people in uniform here,' Vicki remarked. 'Even nurses.'

'Mm. I'm glad we wore ours.' Jancy pushed a stray strand of chestnut hair back under her cap. 'Let's find the others. They're bound to be near the bar.'

They made their way through the crowd, attracting quite a few appreciative glances from the men they passed. Both girls were tall and slender, moving with an easy, confident grace, but it was the masculineness of their uniforms that added an extra touch of erotic sex appeal.

'There they are.' Jancy pointed and glanced back at Vicki, but as she turned to go on she bumped slap into a man who had just turned away from the bar, his hands full of drinks.

'Hey, look out!' Beer slopped out of one of the glasses and splashed on to his uniform.

'Oh, sorry!' Jancy exclaimed automatically, but then saw the three rings on his sleeve, one narrow between two broader, denoting a squadron leader. And on his left breast were the two wings of a pilot. 'Sorry, *sir*,' she amended.

'Good job you're not a navigator,' the officer said with a grin.

Jancy glanced up at him, which was a small surprise in itself; most men she looked straight in the eye if not down on. She liked what she saw: a high-cheekboned face with no spare flesh; alert, vital grey eyes. But there was no time to look further because Vicki was pulling at her sleeve, eager to join the others, so she merely gave a brief nod and allowed herself to be pulled away.

There were half a dozen other people in their party, four men and two girls, all in uniform, although the two men who were waiting for Jancy and Vicki wore the paler khaki of GIs. Soon they were all dancing, not only with their escorts, but swapping partners among their group, the time racing along as they drank and talked between numbers. The place was so crowded that it would have been difficult to find anyone you were looking for, but once, when the drummer went into a terrific solo that was impossible to dance to, Jancy found herself standing only a yard or so away from the squadron leader. She didn't notice him at first, but became aware of someone watching her and turned her head to look into a pair of immediately recognisable grey eyes. Their glances held for a long moment, but then Jancy smiled faintly before looking back at the stage, clapping her hands to the beat.

After that, she noticed the tall, blue-uniformed figure several times more. He, too, seemed to be with a party of people in a mixture of uniforms, and she saw him dancing with two or three different girls, his cap pushed to the back of his head, revealing thick dark hair that almost reached his collar; much too long for a serving officer, but then, these fly-boys could get away with anything.

At nine-thirty the band stopped for a well-earned rest and their place was taken by a much smaller group on the other stage. 'Hey, they're selling American hot-dogs,' someone announced, and the men in their party went off to join the queue to buy some. Jancy went to the ladies' room but on the way back came to a startled standstill as the shriek of an air-raid siren shrilled through the hall, followed by the unmistakable crump of an exploding bomb.

'Take cover! Take cover!' Two air-raid wardens in their black uniforms and helmets came running into the hall shouting and blowing whistles as the ack-ack guns began to fire outside.

Jancy stood indecisively for a moment then turned to head back to her friends, but a man grabbed her arm and ran with her through the mob of scurrying people all making for shelter. They reached the side of the hall and the man pushed her down under one of the tables, then got under himself. Breathless but laughing, Jancy pushed her hat back on her head and turned to thank her rescuer—and wasn't a hundred per cent surprised to find he wore a squadron leader's uniform and had clear grey eyes.

'Thanks. You've obviously done this kind of thing before.'

'When a man tells you to take cover, I don't hesitate,' he returned with mock cowardice.

'Is that how you got the DFC?' Jancy asked, her fingertip flicking the ribbon on his chest.

He grinned. 'Sheer fluke.' Then he nodded towards where she'd been standing with the others. 'I see you go for our Yankee friends.'

'I can't resist the nylons,' she answered flippantly. Another explosion sounded nearby and she covered her ears. Smoke started to permeate the hall and the air-raid warden yelled out for people to put their gas masks on. 'That was close. How long do these raids usually last?'

'Not too long. Not frightened, are you?' he asked, and put his arm round her.

Jancy smiled but leaned back against his arm. 'Haven't you got a gas mask?'

'Lost the thing years ago. Aren't you going to tell me your name?'

She raised her eyebrows. 'Is that an order, sir?'

'Definitely.'

'In that case it's Jancy, Jancy Bruce.'

'Bruce—that sounds Scottish.'

'I think my family were, way back, but they moved south of the border a few centuries ago.'

She raised a questioning eyebrow and he said, 'And mine's Duncan Lyle—but I'm not a Scot either, despite the name. I was named after a friend of my father's.' He grinned at her. 'I can see we're going to have a lot in common.'

Smoke drifted across to them and Jancy coughed.

'It's getting worse; you'd better put your mask on,' Duncan suggested, indicating the case that hung from a strap over her shoulder.

Jancy looked rueful. 'Actually I'm using it as a handbag.'

His eyes narrowing, Duncan said, 'I could put you on a charge for that.'

'And will you?' she asked with a sidelong glance from long-lashed green eyes.

'Perhaps I could be persuaded not to.'

'What would I have to do?'

'I'll think of something.'

'Oh, please, sir,' Jancy said in mock fear. 'I'm only a poor little WRAF. Please don't get me into trouble. Our wing commander is a real old battleaxe.'

He laughed in rich amusement and reached up to take off her hat. Her thick hair, the colour of burnished chestnuts, was drawn up into a loose knot and several strands fell across her cheeks. 'If you have the temper that's supposed to go with green eyes and red hair then I feel sorry for the battleaxe,' he commented.

Above their heads the sound of the ack-ack guns grew louder, then stopped, and into the silence came the shrilling wail of a diving plane, plummeting out of control towards the ground. The noise filled their ears and Duncan drew Jancy tighter, holding her head against his shoulder as it came ever nearer. Then there was an almighty crash as the plane hit, its residue of bombs going up with it. For a few moments after- wards there was dead silence in the hall, then the all- clear sounded and the band immediately began to play 'American Patrol'. Someone began to cheer and soon everyone was joining in as they got to their feet and emerged from what shelter they had managed to find.

Duncan helped Jancy out from under the table but kept a hand on her arm. 'How about giving the British forces a try?' he said quizzically.

She hesitated, but more out of a guilt-feeling about her escort than anything else. After a moment she nodded. 'Why not?'

He danced well, swinging her into a fast quickstep, weaving in and out of the other dancers, making her laugh as she clung to him. And when the dance ended he kept his arm firmly round her waist, drawing her to him as the band went into a slow number. The lights dimmed and Duncan's lips brushed her hair. 'Are you stationed in London?'

Jancy smiled. 'You could say that.'

'May I see you back to your barracks?'

'And what about my GI?'

'Oh, he can see himself home.'

She gave a delighted laugh but said, 'I don't know you.'

'This is wartime,' Duncan pointed out. 'I could get killed tomorrow.'

'Aaah,' she said with mock sympathy. 'Now where have I heard that one before?'

'I can see you're going to be a very hard-hearted woman,' he complained. 'Now what can I do to make you take pity on me?' His left eyebrow rose devilishly. 'How about this?' And he bent to take her lips with his.

As a first kiss given in very adverse conditions it wasn't bad at all. After a few moments Jancy forgot to keep on moving and stood still, letting the other dancers eddy around them, her senses dissolving under the sensual awareness of his kiss. When he lifted his head she slowly opened her eyes and stared into Duncan's.

'I do, very much, want to take you home, Jancy,' he said softly.

She blinked. 'I'm—I'm with a friend,' she temporised.

'Stop making excuses.' He tilted his head to one side assessingly. 'I could always make it an order...'

'Wouldn't that be taking advantage of the situation?' she said with a smile.

'Of course. Isn't that what a good officer is supposed to do?'

She capitulated then, as she'd known she would. 'All right.' And moved closer into his arms.

They danced together for the rest of the evening, although Jancy left him for a short time while she went to square it with her GI escort. He wasn't very happy, of course, but he wasn't a steady boyfriend, just one of the crowd, and as Jancy had bought her own ticket there wasn't much he could do about it.

Vicki listened unashamedly and afterwards grabbed Jancy's arm. 'Let's go to the ladies'.'

'I know what you're going to say,' Jancy said as soon as they were alone. 'That it isn't safe to let someone pick you up at a place like this. But I really like him. He's—somehow special.'

'Are you going to let him take you home?' And when Jancy nodded, 'You're mad! He could be anybody. Promise me you won't let him into your flat.'

'Vicki! I'm not a child. I'm twenty-three years old and I know what I'm doing.'

'You said that about the last man you dated and it turned out to be a disaster,' her friend pointed out ruthlessly. 'Forget him, Jancy.'

'No! He's—I don't know—different.'

'Oh, lord, not *different*! Now I know you're heading for trouble.'

Jancy laughed. 'Don't be ridiculous. I'll be fine.'

She went to rejoin Duncan, her hair tidy under her hat again. He was leaning against a pillar in the dance-hall, his jacket open, his hands casually in his pockets. But the casual air was deceptive, vanishing the moment he moved, his body full of energetic life. She paused for a moment, studying his sharply defined profile, his level brows and clean-cut good looks. He must be about thirty, she guessed, possibly even a year or two older. And he projected an air of confidence and optimism that Jancy had noticed before in men who had done well by an early age. It made her wonder what he did as a profession and she asked him as soon as she got a chance.

The band was playing a really fast number and many couples were trying to jitterbug, much to the amusement of the watching crowd, but Jancy said firmly that there was no way she was going to try it.

'What a relief,' Duncan exclaimed. 'Let's have a drink instead.'

Jancy ordered a gin and tonic but Duncan stuck to a weak shandy. 'Are you flying tonight?' she asked with amusement.

'No, but I've a heavy day tomorrow.'

'What do you do—in civvy street?'

'I work for the family firm. And you?'

She hesitated, then said, 'I do a spot of modelling.'

His gaze sharpened as she knew it would, but then he surprised her. 'I had an idea you might have quite a figure under all that blue blanket material. As a matter of fact I do a lot of painting; I spent quite a long time at art school studying the human form.'

'You're an artist?'

He shook his head regretfully. 'It's only a hobby, I'm afraid. I don't have as much time to spend on it as I'd like.'

'It's this war,' she said, her eyes mischievous.

Duncan grinned back at her. 'Ah, yes, the war.' And clinked his glass against hers as he held her gaze.

It was gone one in the morning before they left. The band had closed on 'We'll Meet Again', and the dancers, thoroughly maudlin by now, had all joined in as they clung to their partners and moved slowly round the floor. Jancy said goodnight to her friends and got another warning from Vicki, but hardly bothered to listen as she walked back to where Duncan was waiting for her.

He put his arm round her waist as they walked out
of the dance-hall. The blackout curtains were pulled
back now and outside the stars shone in a clear sky.
'My car's parked down a side street,' Duncan told her
and led her across the road.

At the corner Jancy paused to glance back. The
sandbags were still outside the door of the dance-hall,
but above them the sign 'Hammersmith Palais' flashed
in brightly coloured lights. And underneath a large
notice which read, 'Tonight—Charity D-Day Anni-
versary Celebration. Come in Uniform or 40s Dress'.

Duncan's car was a Jaguar. Jancy took off her hat
and tossed it in the back, then leaned against the seat
feeling pleasantly tired but excited, too. She told
Duncan where she lived, in a mews flat in Kensington,
and he needed no directions as he drove confidently
through the London streets. She glanced at his lean
profile, remembering Vicki's warning and wondering
whether to ask him in for a drink. Whether to play
it cool or to give way to this mounting excitement and
anticipation.

Her own feelings surprised her; she hadn't felt this
way after meeting a new man for ages. Perhaps it had
been the wartime nostalgia trip that had done it; a
throw-back to the 'live for today because there might
be no tomorrow' lifestyle. There must have been an
urgency to life then, she thought musingly. No time
for long courtships; you had to make up your mind
about your feelings and take what happiness you could
get.

They pulled up at a traffic-light and Duncan turned
to look at her. 'What are you thinking?' he asked,
seeing her pensive expression.

'About the war. I know it was a terrible time—but it must have been an exhilarating time too, in some ways. And for some people.'

He nodded. 'The adrenalin must have really been flowing. I doubt if there are many experiences to compare with it now.'

The lights changed to green and he drove on for a short way before pulling into the road that led to Jancy's mews. She told him where to stop but didn't hurry to get out of the car. 'Where did you get your uniform?'

'It belonged to my great-uncle. He had quite a war, evidently. Was shot down in the drink three times before he finally bought it in 1943.' Unknowingly Duncan used the wartime slang.

'So the wings were his?'

'Yes, and the medals.' Duncan lifted his hand to touch the ribbons. 'I've an idea he would have approved of me wearing his uniform tonight— especially as it led to meeting you. He was quite a man for the girls, by all accounts.'

'And are you?'

He grinned. 'Depends on the girl.' Lifting his hand he gently brushed her cheek, his touch feather-light, the grin fading as he looked at her intently. 'Do we say goodnight here—or are you going to ask me in for a drink?'

'Just for a drink?' Jancy asked, testing him.

He nodded. 'Just for a drink.'

Her flat was feminine but not intensely so. Built out of what had once been a stable over a coach-house, it was all on one floor and wasn't terribly large, just a big sitting-room at the front, and bedroom, bathroom and tiny kitchen at the back. But it was all that Jancy needed and was in a good area: close to a fashionable shopping centre, the Albert Hall for concerts, a Tube station, and Kensington Palace Gardens when she felt like getting back to nature.

Duncan looked round approvingly and crossed to look at her collection of framed prints on one of the side walls. 'Did you pick these yourself?'

'Yes. I bought most of them from dealers but a couple I found in a flea market.'

'You have good taste,' he observed. 'And you've made a good investment.'

His compliment pleased her far more than if he'd praised her looks. Jancy was used to having men flatter her; it was all part of being a model, and she had become rather blasé about it. But because she was a model she was also objective about her looks. She knew she was attractive, her hair and her figure being her best assets. But she wasn't beautiful. Her features weren't perfect enough for that, her nose being a little too retroussé and her mouth too wide when she smiled, which she did—often. But her figure *was* good. Tall, slender and softly rounded in all the right places, and she made sure she kept it that way with plenty of exercise and a regular diet. So there was always work for someone with her glowing hair, her figure and that attractive smile.

She smiled at Duncan now. 'Thank you. You obviously know quite a bit about prints.'

'It was one of the subjects we had to study at art college.'

'Oh, of course. I'd forgotten. What would you like to drink?'

Again he surprised her. 'A coffee would be nice.'

He followed her into the kitchen while she made it and leaned against the door-jamb. 'You haven't told me yet whether you have a temper,' he reminded her.

Jancy laughed. 'I don't often have occasion to get angry.'

'No, I don't suppose you do. What kind of model are you?'

'Every kind: clothes, photographic, whatever work I can get. So's Vicki—the girl I was with tonight.' She handed him his coffee and they went back into the sitting-room.

'And do you sit for artists?' Duncan asked, sitting in an armchair and stretching out his long legs.

She shook her head. 'No, I've never been asked.'

'And if I asked you?'

'That would depend.'

'On what?'

'On just how you wanted me to pose—and whether you could afford my rates, of course,' she said lightly, but with a little wariness in her voice.

Duncan gave her a lazy grin. 'I've got past the stage of painting nudes, if that's what you're thinking. I'm not that kind of artist.'

'So what kind of artist are you?'

'Oh, I do all the traditional stuff: portraits, landscapes, to keep my hand in; but I also do a few surrealistic pieces. I'll show you my work some time and you can see how you feel about it.'

In his voice there was a quiet confidence that they would be seeing a great deal more of each other in the future, and Jancy found that she liked the idea a lot. They went on talking about art, discovering each other's likes and dislikes, but Jancy soon found out that Duncan knew far more than she did. Not that he pushed his knowledge down her throat—if anything he was slightly reticent—but she was discerning enough to recognise his love of the subject. She made more coffee, but when Duncan had finished his second cup he reluctantly looked at his watch and stood up. 'I'm afraid I have to go; as I said, I've a heavy day tomorrow—or rather today.'

'Doing what?' Jancy asked as she lazily uncoiled herself from the settee.

'I'm an architect in my father's firm, and I have to meet a client at nine-thirty on a site near Canterbury. Otherwise...' He smiled and took her arm to draw her towards him. 'Otherwise I could stay and talk all night.'

Reaching up he took the clips from her hair, watching in fascination as it tumbled down about her shoulders and halfway down her back. 'I want to paint you, Coppernob,' he said thickly, and put his hands in her hair as he kissed her, his shoulders hunching as the kiss deepened and became demanding.

It was a while before he drew away, but he didn't push it, instead asking for her phone number in a voice that wasn't completely steady, then saying, 'Goodnight,' and leaving immediately afterwards.

Duncan rang the next evening and asked her out to dinner, the first of many dates in which they gradually explored each other's character and liked what they learned. It was an unhurried courtship, both of them knowing that it was very special and wanting to savour each new phase of their relationship. Not for them an immediate plunge into an intensely sexual affair. As the days passed they both grew more certain that what they had was going to be for keeps. They were falling in love; it was as simple as that. And they both knew that when the time came for them to go to bed together it would have to be just right so that they could look back on it as the most wonderful time in their lives.

Jancy often had to go away to do modelling assignments, and Duncan's work, too, often took him away, sometimes for weeks at a time, but he took her to his flat-cum-studio in Highgate and showed her his paintings. His traditional-style paintings, mostly watercolours, were good, even Jancy's untrained eye could see that, but his surrealist pictures were something else again. All Jancy had seen in the genre were photographs of Salvador Dali's works, but Duncan's, although he took familiar objects and transformed them, weren't so hard or brilliantly coloured. He had a picture of a wall of stones, but when you looked closely the stones were box-like houses piled on top of one another with windows where people beat against the glass trying to get out.

'Wow! What gave you the idea for that?'

'Seeing all the housing estates taking over the landscape; just hundreds of houses all the same and squeezed into the smallest available space.' He looked at the picture moodily for a moment. 'I'm not happy with it, of course. It isn't what I'm trying to find, the style I want to use.'

Jancy straightened up from where she'd been kneeling on the floor to take a closer look at the painting. 'You must keep trying,' she said with certainty. 'I know you'll find what you're looking for.'

Putting his arm round her, Duncan said huskily, 'That doesn't seem so important any more.' And he kissed her neck.

Jancy leaned back against him in delicious sen-
suality, but said, 'You said you wanted to paint me.'

'And I still do. Will you let me?'

She turned to put her arms round his neck, smiling
into his eyes. 'Yes.'

'When?'

'Whenever you like.'

He painted her not in his conventional style, but
as he saw her with his surrealist eye. He painted her
as a tree. Her feet became roots, her knee a ridge in
the trunk, and he clothed her in brown material that
under his hands became the detailed roughness of
bark. Her upspread arms became branches, and the
long tresses of her hair spread out around her head
in a glorious autumn tracery of delicate leaves and
foliage dappled by the sun. Her skin he had coloured
as the bark and leaves so that she melted into them,
but all her facial features were there and he had given
her the haunting loveliness of a dryad. And in a split
in the trunk he had painted in her left breast with an
exquisite pleasure that showed.

It had taken several weeks to paint the picture and
when she had first posed for him Jancy had been
modest and kept on her bra under the brown material,
but Duncan had frowned. 'Your straps show; take that
thing off.' And he had impatiently come round to do
it himself and cast the lacy garment aside. 'That's
better.' He'd fussed around with the material, getting
it just how he wanted it and, before Jancy could
protest, had torn a long rent in it to reveal her breast.

'Hey!'

He'd given her an abstracted look and then grinned.
'You don't mind, do you?' And he'd bent to kiss her

breast until the nipple stood proud and pouting. 'Now, that's how I'd like to paint it.'

He had walked over to his easel and begun to draw, working on until Jancy had complained that her arms ached. Then he'd come over and slipped the brown tweed over her head, drawing her down on to a couch where he'd kissed and caressed her, telling her how beautiful her body was, how perfect.

On the day the painting was finished Duncan took her out to celebrate, thrilled and happy that he had found the style he was looking for, knowing that it was the best thing he'd ever done. And it was that night they went to bed together for the first time. The evening had been very special, electric with anticipation, both of them aware that the time was right. They dined in what had become their favourite restaurant, and danced well past midnight, holding each other close, knowing that in a short while they would make love.

They went back to Duncan's studio and Jancy stood in front of the painting as he took off her clothes, loving her with his lips and his hands as he did so, making her moan in an aching agony of desire. 'I love you, Coppernob,' he told her heatedly. 'I love every part of you. Your sweet face, your exquisite body. Your hair, your beautiful breasts.' Lifting his hands he put them on either side of her head. 'Marry me, my darling. Please say yes.'

Jancy never did actually say yes; she didn't have to. She just gave a cry of happiness and reached up to kiss him, kiss him so ardently that Duncan swept her up and carried her into his bedroom. They made love at first with passionate abandon and later with deep tenderness, each striving to please the other and delighting in this consummation of a love that they knew would last forever.

'Sweetheart,' Duncan murmured against her neck, his need for the moment satiated. 'You must come down and meet my family. Then we'll get officially engaged.' Propping himself up on his elbow, he added eagerly, 'When I was down in Kent I saw this old oast-house that could be converted into a marvellous home for us.'

'Oast-house?' The lamp was still on and by its light Jancy traced her fingertips across his broad, smooth chest.

'It's an old kiln where they used to dry hops to make beer.'

'You want us to live in an oven!'

He laughed. 'Idiot.' Lowering his head he circled her nipple with his tongue. 'Do you know I'm crazy about your breasts?'

'I had noticed.' But she pushed him away. 'Tell me some more about this oast-house.'

'Well, it's in a beautiful piece of unspoilt country-side just a few miles from Canterbury and has about half an acre of ground. It will need quite a lot of work to convert it into a house, of course, but once it's done I know that you'll love it. And it will be fun to do, together. You'd like to live in the country rather than London, wouldn't you? It would be quite easy to commute from there.'

'It sounds wonderful.' A thought occurred to her. 'But I already have a house in the country.' And she chuckled at his surprised look. 'You didn't know I was a woman of property, did you? It's just a small cottage on the Yorkshire moors. It belonged to my great-aunt, my grandfather's sister. She never married because her fiancé was killed in the war, and she bought this cottage for holidays. It's miles from anywhere, but the scenery is fantastic: all wild, rolling hills covered in heather. She should have left it to my father, I suppose, because he was her nearest relative, but she disapproved of my parents splitting up, so she left it to me instead.'

'Do you go there much?'

Jancy shook her head rather ruefully. 'It's such a long way from London; I never seem to find the time.' She smiled at him. 'But maybe *we'll* go there some time. I think Aunt Cecily would have approved of you.'

But Duncan wasn't really listening. His eyes had darkened as he began to explore her again, his hands fondling and stroking. Jancy gave a small gasp of pain as his fingers closed on her breast in a sudden sharpening of desire.

'Sorry, didn't mean to hurt.' But his voice was thick as he rolled on top of her and began to make love yet again.

Jancy had already met Duncan's father once, when she had picked Duncan up from his office one evening when his car was in the garage for a service, but she had yet to meet his mother and married sister. They lived in Surrey, in the commuter belt, in a pleasant Edwardian house near the golf course that was Duncan's father's main leisure interest. And his sister lived with her accountant husband only a few miles away. Duncan took her down on the following Sunday, Jancy sitting rather nervously beside him, knowing that a lot depended on today. She was afraid that his parents might disapprove of his marrying a model, that they might want him to marry a girl with a less public career.

They hadn't told his family that they were engaged—Duncan intended to announce it over lunch—but Duncan's mother took one look at her son's expression of buoyant happiness and guessed immediately. They couldn't have been more kind, making Jancy very welcome, and full of excitement at the thought of a coming wedding. 'I was beginning to think that Duncan would never find the right girl,' Mrs Lyle confided. 'But I'm so pleased he's found someone as lovely as you.'

Lunch was one of the happiest meals Jancy had ever experienced. Duncan's sister, Olivia, was there with her husband Jack and little daughter Chantal—who begged Jancy to promise faithfully that she could be a bridesmaid.

'Jancy might have nieces of her own that she wants for bridesmaids,' her mother reproved her.

But Jancy shook her head, her eyes clouding a little. 'I don't have any brothers or sisters. My parents split up when I was quite young and they've both married again and live abroad. I have two older stepbrothers from the woman my father married, but I've only ever seen them a couple of times, so I would be very happy for Chantal to be a bridesmaid.'

The little girl clapped her hands in delight. 'When? And what colour dress can I have?'

Everyone laughed and Duncan scooped her up on his knee. 'Not for ages yet, I'm afraid, little one. Jancy has a modelling assignment in Greece shortly, and then I have to go to New Zealand for the company, possibly for a couple of months.'

His eyes met Jancy's across the table and they exchanged a rueful look. She had known that he had to go to New Zealand of course, but his departure hadn't seemed so near or two months so long until now. Her heart filled with anticipated loneliness, a precursor of the aching emptiness she knew she would always feel in future when they were apart. Her eyes fell to the child on his lap. Maybe in time she wouldn't be so lonely; she was sure that Duncan would make a wonderful father. But she didn't want children too soon, she decided; she would like at least a couple of years of having Duncan to herself first.

The following weekend they drove down to Kent to see the oast-house. It was a perfect late summer day, still and cloudless, the countryside rich and green, not yet turning into the flame of autumn. After turning off the main road, they drove through a couple of small, idyllic villages, past a series of hop fields, and then down a rutted lane until a farm gate barred their way. 'Let's walk from here,' Duncan suggested.

Taking her hand, he led her through the gate, and into a walled yard, then stopped and watched for her reaction as Jancy took her first look at the oast-house. It was very dilapidated but the main structure was still there: two round towers in warm red brick topped by conical wooden roofs on top of which were dunce's-cap-shaped cauls. The towers were attached to a gabled building at their rear but this had lost its roof completely and its windows were broken and rotten. But Jancy, too, could see its potential and she gave him a glowing look before running closer.

'Can we go inside? Is it safe?' She explored excitedly, giving an exclamation of delight at the view from the back of the building, over a meadow to an orchard that in the spring would be a mass of apple blossom, and beyond to where the spire of a distant church rose above the trees.

'I thought we could have a sitting-room with one wall almost entirely of glass at the back of the house, and have a kitchen in the right-hand tower with a guest room and bathroom above it.' Duncan began to draw plans on a sheet of paper attached to a clipboard with Jancy throwing in eager suggestions and enthusiastic approval.

But then she caught his hand. 'Hey, we haven't even got the place yet. It may not be for sale.'

Sticking the pencil behind his ear, Duncan put his arms round her waist, grinning down at her. 'It is for sale. I made enquiries when I was down here before.'

'But we might not be able to afford it.'

'We can. As a matter of fact I've put a deposit on it.'

'You have? When?'

'Three weeks ago.'

'But that was before you asked me to marry you!' He gave a huge grin and Jancy punched him in the chest. 'You were that sure of me, huh?'

Duncan's arms tightened as his eyes grew intense. 'I knew that I was falling in love with you and that I wanted you for my wife. Finding this place and being able to buy it seemed an omen for the future. I only hoped and prayed that you felt the same. I want everything to be perfect for us, Jancy. I want to build you a beautiful house that will be a fit setting for someone as lovely as you.'

Reaching into his pocket, he took out a small box and slid the ring inside on to her engagement finger. It was a solitaire rose diamond, beautifully cut, that caught the sun and fractured it into a thousand brilliant rainbows as she moved her hand.

'Oh, Duncan! It—it's just beautiful!' Tears came to her eyes and she put her arms round his neck to hug him, thinking that this was one of the best days of her life.

But presently Duncan made it even better. He led her through the overgrown garden to the meadow beyond and pulled her down to lie beside him in the long green grass. Away from all eyes, he made love to her there, the sun hot on their naked bodies, the scent of wild flowers in their nostrils, birdsong and the buzz of a contented bee the only sounds other than their panting breath.

The next couple of weeks were busy ones for them both, Jancy doing an assignment for a mail order fashion magazine, and Duncan drawing up the plans for the oast-house conversion and also starting another painting of her. But then they had to part, knowing it would be for almost three months as Jancy would still be in Greece when Duncan had to leave for New Zealand. They had one last, very rapturous night of love before he took her to the airport, each promising to write and telephone as often as they could.

'And we'll set a wedding date as soon as I get back,' Duncan said firmly.

She smiled mistily. 'Is that a promise?'

'No, a threat,' he said, grinning.

Jancy missed him almost at once, even though she was kept busy with her work and had the members of a large crew for company. She missed little things like walking with him, her hand in his or his arm familiarly round her waist. She missed, too, that look

of possessiveness and pride that had come into his
face since they had become lovers. The other models
pulled her leg when they found her with a rapt
expression on her face, her thoughts back in England.
Jancy laughed with them, but longed for the time
when she and Duncan could be together for keeps.

It was when she had been in Greece for almost three
weeks that she first noticed that the skin of her left
nipple had drawn up into a small pucker. At first she
dismissed it, and not being narcissistic about her own
body didn't bother to look at it again. But she was
sharing a room with another model and one day, when
she was changing, the other girl also noticed it.

'I'd get a doctor to look at that, if I were you,' the
girl commented.

Surprised, Jancy went to look at herself in the
mirror and frowned; it might have been her imagination, but the skin seemed to have drawn back even
further in just a few days. That night she rang Duncan
to say goodbye to him before he left for New Zealand.
She almost mentioned about her nipple, but something held her back: he was always telling her how
perfect she was and her female pride didn't want to
detract from that image, especially when he was going
away. Anyway, it was probably nothing; probably
came from sunbathing topless when she wasn't used
to it.

But she was sufficiently uneasy to go to her doctor
as soon as she got back to England, and was made
even more uneasy when she sent Jancy for an
immediate X-ray and got her an appointment with a
consultant at an oncology clinic.

After examining her the consultant, a man in his
mid-forties who looked as if he worked too hard, said,

'It could be that you have an infection behind the nipple, but I shall have to do a biopsy to find out.'

'A biopsy?' Jancy looked at him in trepidation.

'That's a small exploratory operation. Nothing very terrible. You'll only have to be in hospital overnight.'

'Will—will there be much of a scar?'

He looked at her assessingly under his brows and shook his head. 'No, it will be lost in the corona around the nipple. When can you come in?'

Jancy gave a small sigh of relief and smiled at him. 'Any time.'

'Good. How about the day after tomorrow?'

She was rather taken aback that he wanted to do it so quickly; it wasn't as if she was a private patient or anything. 'Yes. OK.'

She was booked into a big London teaching hospital and somewhat to her surprise was given a small private room off the main women's surgical ward. She went alone; Vicki was away on an assignment, and it seemed silly to ask one of her other friends to go with her for such a trivial thing. In fact it had all happened so quickly that she hadn't even bothered to tell anyone. Jancy had brought one of her own nightgowns with her but rather ruefully swapped it for the hospital gown and cap. Always having been extremely healthy all her life, she had never been in hospital before and was naturally rather nervous. But the nurses were reassuring and she went down to the operating theatre with hardly a qualm.

It was a few hours later when she woke, feeling dry and thirsty and still rather woozy from the anaesthetic. There was a dressing on her breast but it hardly hurt at all, thankfully. When the sister came in to see her Jancy asked how the op had gone, but the nurse said that they were still waiting for the lab results. And she had to wait until the evening when the consultant came to see her before she heard.

He had been through the same experience too many times to waste time or words by trying to soften the blow. He just said, 'We've had the results of the lab test. I'm afraid you have a cancer.' And as Jancy stared at him with suddenly terrified eyes, 'You will have to have a mastectomy.'

'You—you mean . . .?'

'Yes. Complete removal of the left breast.'

CHAPTER TWO

FOR a few seconds Jancy's stunned brain wouldn't work, but then she said sharply, 'You mean a lumpectomy—just the removal of the lump?'

But he shook his head. 'No, it's too far gone for that. It will have to be the full operation.'

She stared at him, still hardly able to take it in, but then anger filled her mind in an overwhelming flood of protest. 'You're wrong! You've made a mistake. I can't possibly have cancer. I'm only twenty-three! It's older women who get breast cancer.'

'I'm sorry, there's no doubt. It's the——'

'I tell you you're wrong!' she interrupted fiercely. 'I want a second opinion.'

'You're entitled to that, of course,' the consultant said wearily. 'I'll come and see you again first thing in the morning and we'll talk about it then.' He placed a hand on her shoulder. 'It's hard to take, I know. But you've been found to have a cancerous growth and it will have to be removed to save your life.'

It was those last few words that penetrated Jancy's fragile wall of disbelief. She had cancer. She could die. He went out and closed the door behind him, leaving her staring blindly across the room, her world in shreds. 'No! No!' She screamed out the words, beating her fists against the bed, trying to fight against fate, trying to drive away the awful truth by sheer will-power. Tears streamed from her eyes, and her

31

mouth set into a rigid scream of defiance as she shouted out again, 'No! No! No!'

A sister and a nurse hurried in, caught her flailing arms and tried to calm her. But Jancy pushed them away and tried to get out of bed, sobbing wildly. 'It isn't true. They've made a mistake. I'm going home.'

In the end they gave her an injection that sedated her, although it didn't knock her out completely. From time to time during that long night she would almost surface, her brain in a frenzy, knowing that something terrible was about to happen to her. She tossed restlessly from side to side and moaned when she felt a pain in her breast. Her breast—yes, that was it, they were going to do something to her breast. But they couldn't do that. Duncan loved her breasts; loved to kiss and fondle them, loved to paint them. Duncan wouldn't let anyone hurt her. He would take care of her.

That thought, deep in her subconscious as it was, gave Jancy some comfort and she fell asleep at last, but woke again with the early morning noises of the hospital. She stirred, feeling heavy-headed and sluggish, but then felt a twinge of pain from the wound in her breast, making memory come flooding back. Oh, no! Oh, please, no. Don't let it be true, she prayed. But the sympathetic eyes of the nurse who came in to see her denied her prayers. 'Do you feel up to some breakfast?' she asked.

Jancy shook her head. 'No.'

'Still feeling queasy?'

'No,' Jancy said irritably. 'I just don't want anything.'

The nurse raised the head of the bed and Jancy leaned back against the pillows, feeling drained. But gradually her mind began to work, recalling maga-zine articles about breast cancer that she'd only glanced at in idle curiosity because it could never happen to her. Surely they'd said that it wasn't necessary to have an operation, that you could have radiotherapy instead? And then there were implants; you could have those too, so that when you woke from the operation you didn't look any different. Her spirits began to rise and she went to the basin to wash and put on some make-up.

The consultant came back early, giving a small sigh when he saw the light of battle in her eyes. Without giving her a chance to speak, he said, 'The lab tests on your biopsy were done twice; I insisted on that because of your youth. There can be absolutely no doubt that your tumour is a cancer.'

'You couldn't possibly have mixed my results up with anyone else's?' Jancy demanded.

He shook his head wryly, having expected the question.

'All right.' She bit her lip, accepting the diagnosis. 'In that case I'll have radiotherapy to get rid of it instead of an operation.'

Again he shook his head. 'I'm afraid that there isn't any choice. It's the kind of tumour that could have been there for some time and has only just manifested itself. An operation is the only option.'

Jancy's face whitened and she gripped the sheets tightly. 'Are you absolutely sure? If there's any other way at all, then I'll take it. Even if it means all my hair will fall out...' Her voice trailed off as she saw him shake his head yet again. Blinking hard to keep back the tears, she went on unsteadily, 'In that case

I'll have an implant at the same time as the operation so that——'

'I'm sorry, it can't be done. I don't know how much I may have to cut away—not with your type of cancer. And I certainly don't recommend having the breast restructured until two years after the operation at the earliest.'

'But you must! You must, do you understand? I have some money; I can pay. Or if you can't do it then get someone who can.' Her voice rose to the point of hysteria.

'It isn't a question of payment. It just isn't a treatment I can possibly recommend,' he returned patiently. 'If the cancer recurs——'

'You mean it can come back?' She stared at him with frightened eyes.

'It's unlikely after two years, and after five years you should be OK.'

Despair filled her heart. 'Oh, God, there must be some other way. There must be some other way.'

But yet again he shook his head.

The hairline cracks in the ceiling formed themselves into the face of a deformed devil, long-nosed and scowling, and with vicious horns. Jancy had never noticed the cracks on the ceiling before but now she lay on her bed at home and stared up at them, her eyes wide and unblinking. Deformed. The word stayed in her brain. That's what I shall be: deformed, ugly. I won't be able to work—whoever heard of a model with only one breast! Or a bride, come to that. Her mind kept coming back to that thought although she tried to push it away. She remembered Duncan fondling her, telling her how much he loved her body.

But would he still love it when it was deformed, disfigured?

Sudden despair filled her again and Jancy began to cry in great, agonised sobs, her arms wrapped round herself, keening as in the depths of grief. But then rage turned inwards and she began to hit herself, hating her own body for betraying her. 'Why me?' she cried out. 'Why me? What have I done?' She would have liked someone to talk to, then, a shoulder to cry on. But it was a weekday and everyone she knew would be at work. Vicki, in fact, was in France for a fashion show and wouldn't be back until next week, when Jancy would be in hospital again having the operation. The mastectomy. She could hardly bring herself to say the word. But even that sounded better than breast cancer or amputation.

Daylight faded into evening and she forced herself to get up and make a coffee, still feeling unable to eat. Her whole life was in pieces and she could see no way in which she could put them together. At least not for two years. In two years she could have her breast reconstructed. But what was she supposed to do in the meantime? Even supposing she lived that long, she thought bitterly. But no, she must be positive, think positive. Wasn't that what the sister at the hospital had told her? It was all right for her to say it; she was married and pushing forty-five, not twenty-three years old, single, and with her whole life in ruins!

Anger alternated with despair for the rest of that day. Jancy had told her agency that she wouldn't be available for work for a couple of days, without bothering to tell them why. But the next morning she had to bring herself to ring them again and cancel all the work they had lined up for her, and tell them that she wouldn't be available indefinitely. 'But why?' they wanted to know. 'What's happened?'

But Jancy couldn't bring herself to tell them. 'It's a—a personal matter,' she muttered, and hastily rang off.

The phone rang almost immediately and she guessed that it was the agency wanting more information, but tears were already streaming and she just let the phone ring until they gave up. Then she took the receiver off the hook and left it off all day.

The following day she had to go to the hospital to have an X-ray done of her chest—just as a check, they'd said—and then a bone scan, having to sit and stand in various positions while a huge camera took special photographs of her body and head. The process took quite a while and the technician was young and impressionable. They got chatting and he confided, after seeing her prints on a computer screen, that her bone scan was clear. Which was something at least; Jancy had begun to fear that the consultant hadn't told her everything and that she had cancer really badly. That the news came as a great relief was almost a surprise; but at least it proved to her that she still wanted to live even if she was ugly. But she still felt very low and depressed, ready to burst into tears at the slightest thing.

Duncan had given her a key to his flat and asked her to keep an eye on it while he was away. So that evening, in need of comfort, Jancy drove over to Highgate, parked the car near the famous old cemetery where Karl Marx was buried, and let herself into his flat. The place was so full of Duncan's things, his spirit, that he might almost have been there. She wandered round, touching his clothes, picking up books that he'd left out and putting them back on the shelves, making sure that the kitchen was OK. The place felt cold so she switched on the central heating, programming it to come on for a few hours every evening: it would be November before Duncan came home and she wanted the place to be warm for him.

Putting on one of his favourite records, Debussy's 'Prélude à l'Après-midi d'un Faune', Jancy poured herself a drink and went into Duncan's studio. The new portrait of her stood on the easel, covered by a sheet of white cloth. Throwing it back, she stared at the half-finished picture. This time he was painting her as a stone bust on a pedestal. Bust! Jancy thought with hollow bitterness; that was a cruel irony. But this was a bust that was full of life, her eyes open in the white marble of her face. Emerald-green eyes full of vitality and youth and happiness. Then there was the white column of her neck, her shoulders, and then, just as the swell of her breasts reached the pedestal, Duncan had painted in her nipples, small and pink and rosy, and entirely delectable.

She stood staring at the painting for a long time, slowly reaching out to touch the left nipple, wondering what she would look like when it was all over. Duncan had so loved her body; would he be able to stand the sight of her with only one breast? She tried to imagine how she would tell him, what words she would use to describe what had happened. Would she try to break it gently, or come right out with it as the surgeon had done? But it would have to be the latter way: although it had seemed cruel, she knew that it had been better not to prevaricate. What would Duncan's reaction be? she wondered. Would he find the whole idea repulsive? Would he turn from her in

disgust when he saw the mutilated body that he had
thought so perfect?

But if she told him over the phone then she wouldn't
be able to see his face, would be spared his reaction.
For a few moments the idea was very appealing, but
suddenly Jancy knew that she couldn't do it that way.
If she told him over the phone it would give him time
to prepare himself when he saw her, to school his features so that she wouldn't see how repulsive he found
her—and she was quite sure that he would hate the
sight of her. *Hate the sight of her!* Oh, God, when
they had loved each other so much. It wasn't fair! It
just wasn't fair. Close to tears again, Jancy covered
the picture and went to pour herself another drink.

She sat on Duncan's bed, the bed in which they had
first made love. Forcing herself to concentrate, she
tried to put herself in Duncan's place, to see it from
his point of view. She had no doubt that he would
stand by her, would still marry her; he loved her and
would go on loving her. They would probably even
find some sort of happiness. But it would never be
the same. Their future would never have that bright,
shining promise of perfection that Duncan had so
wanted to give her. And she would always know,
whenever he looked at her, that his artist's eye would
be affronted at the sight of her deformed figure, even
though he hid it. As he would hide it, out of love,
out of pity. The thought of his pity filled her with
desolation.

She had taken a natural pride and pleasure in her
body, in her youth and slimness, and since meeting
Duncan that pride had grown a hundredfold. It was
the greatest gift she had, one which she was so happy
to give him, in love, in marriage. But now all the self-

respect was gone. She was beginning to hate the body that had played such a dirty trick on her, and couldn't imagine Duncan even bearing to look at her without inner revulsion. He would try to avoid looking at her, she thought. Never again would he ask her to pose for him. There would be no more portraits showing her breasts. It wouldn't be so bad when she had clothes on. She would be given a false breast to wear; they had told her that at the hospital. 'No one will know the difference,' they'd said soothingly. But Duncan would know, would be aware of it all the time. And when they were in bed making love—oh, God, he would certainly know then! Unless of course she could hide herself away from him for two years in the hope that she would survive that long and could then have an implant.

The thought came to her with mocking irony, but once it entered her mind it wouldn't go away.

Lying down, Jancy ran her hand over the pillow where he had lain, her thoughts full of the man she loved. She needed him so much now. She felt so lonely and afraid. She wanted to pick up the phone and tell him, knowing that Duncan would catch the next plane and come home to be with her no matter what his feelings. Fleetingly she thought of calling her mother, but she hadn't seen her in years and they had grown so far apart; it would be like asking for comfort from a stranger. Her tired brain couldn't cope with the whirling thoughts and she slept a little, her hand gripping the pillow. It was very late when she left the flat to go home, but when she did Jancy's mind was made up: she wouldn't tell Duncan or anyone, she would face this alone.

He telephoned from New Zealand the next evening. 'Hi, there, darling. How are you?'

'F-fine. And you?'

'Longing to come home. I tried to call you last night but there was no reply.'

'I went round to your flat. It was cold so I put the central heating on.'

'Thanks. Were you there long? I tried to call several times.'

'Yes. I... As a matter of fact I lay down on your bed for a while and I must have fallen asleep.'

Duncan chuckled, his voice sounding achingly close instead of thousands of miles away. 'I wonder what you were thinking about when you were lying on the bed. You couldn't have been missing me, could you?'

A great wave of love and longing engulfed her so that it was hard to speak, but Jancy managed to say as lightly as she could, 'Certainly not. I was just missing my sleep, that's all.'

He gave a mock sigh. 'You're not even pining one little bit?'

'Not even half a little bit.' But her voice was unsteady and heavy with bitten-back tears.

'You sound strange. Are you sure you're all right?' There was concern in his voice.

'Yes, of course,' Jancy lied bravely. 'I'm just—I'm just coming down with a cold, I think.'

'And me not there to look after you. Promise me you'll take çare of yourself. I love and miss you so much, my darling Coppernob.'

'Oh, Duncan.' Her heart filling with a great need for him, Jancy suddenly decided to tell him everything and blurted out, 'Duncan, there's something I have to——'

But he was still speaking. 'I can't wait to get home to see you again, to make love to you. You're so lovely. Every night I lie here wanting you, wishing that we were together, wanting to touch your beautiful body.' His voice had grown husky with desire, but lightened as he went on, 'And I've thought of lots more pictures I want to paint of you. As soon as I get back I'll finish the bust picture and start on another. So take care of yourself, my love, and take care of that gorgeous figure of yours.'

'Yes,' Jancy answered mechanically. 'Yes, of course. And you look after yourself, too. Goodbye, Duncan. L-love you.'

Replacing the receiver, Jancy sat and stared at it for a long time, gradually accepting that she now knew what her future was going to be, what she had to do.

The devastating psychological fears had driven all thoughts of how painful the operation might be from Jancy's mind almost till the last moment, and it was only when she was lying in the hospital on the eve of the operation that she began to be really afraid. But it was nowhere near as bad as she had expected. She came round to find herself attached to drips and drains, and her throat and neck painfully sore, but her left breast just felt numb at first. It was later that she began to feel as if a mailed fist had got hold of the left side of her chest and was squeezing it hard. Her arm, too, felt very painful when she tried to lift it. The wound was covered by such a large dressing that when she looked at it she could almost believe she was still OK. It was when they removed the dressing for the first time, and she saw that the breast was completely gone, that she broke down again. 'Oh,

God!' She turned away, fighting back tears, but the nurse, a girl about her own age, put her arms round her and Jancy gave way to grief for all that she had lost.

The consultant told her he'd had to do a radical mastectomy, taking away not only her breast but also the lymph gland under her arm and the muscles of her chest, which explained why her arm felt so sore.

Jancy was young and she healed quite quickly, far more quickly than an older woman in the next room who'd had the same operation on the same day. She was a buxom middle-aged woman, married and with grown-up children, who didn't seem to mind the operation at all. 'The way I see it,' she said philosophically, 'I've been cured of cancer, and that's all I care about. I want to live to see my grandchildren grow up.' She laughed. 'Do you know what one of the nurses told me when I asked why most women have to have their left breasts off? She said it was because most men were right-handed.'

Jancy stared at her. 'You—you mean, it's caused because men touch you?'

'Oh, I don't suppose so for a minute,' the woman answered, seeing her stricken face. 'It's only a joke. They just don't know what causes it, do they?'

The evening meal was brought round and the woman went back to her flower-filled room to eat it, but Jancy didn't touch hers. Could the demonstration of a man's love do this evil thing to you? she wondered with another wave of bitter hatred against fate. She remembered when she and Duncan had been making love and the pain she had felt when he had inadvertently squeezed her nipple in a moment of passion. Could that have caused the cancer? For a few moments her mind filled with terror, but then she remembered the consultant saying that it had probably been growing inside her for some time, and Jancy felt almost weak with relief. She didn't want anything to taint the memory of the love she'd shared with Duncan; she could even be glad that this terrible thing had been growing inside her for years if it protected her precious memories.

Next time the consultant came to see her she asked him what had caused the tumour but, as usual, he shook his head. 'It's almost impossible to say definitely. It isn't common in a woman as young as you. We're doing research all the time and we're managing to isolate some causes of some kinds of cancers. And we're finding new drugs to treat others, or new ways to treat them, but wiping out cancer completely is still a long way off, I'm afraid.'

He went away and they brought in her lunch, but she didn't eat it. The nurse came to collect her untouched meal and scolded her. 'You've got to eat.'

But Jancy didn't care any more. She felt so wretched and depressed that she didn't want to do anything. The future stretched bleak and empty and she had no courage to face it. They wanted her to see a counsellor from the Mastectomy Association, a woman who had also undergone the operation, but Jancy refused point-blank. She could hardly bring herself to say the word, let alone talk about it with someone else. But she did want to get out of the hospital; she hated the place because they all knew what had happened to her, and she couldn't wait to leave. Lifting her arm was painful, so she didn't bother to do the set of exercises that the physiotherapist gave her, but when the woman said, 'You're not leaving this hos-

pital until you can lift your left hand over your head
and touch your right ear!' Jancy hastily began the
programme.

She finally left the hospital after ten days, with
orders to come back in a month's time to see the consultant. There was no one to take her home, just as
she had had no visitors or flowers during her stay.
How could there be, when she had told no one where
she was going? She took a taxi back to the mews and
wandered from room to room in the flat, somehow
surprised that it was just the same when she felt so
different. But she was grateful to be home.

Jancy sat down in an armchair, already feeling
weary. She would have a couple of days of complete
rest, she decided. A time in which to recoup her
strength before preparing for the course on which
she'd made up her mind with such difficulty and re-
luctance. Leaning back in the chair, she closed her
eyes—but almost immediately the peace was broken
by the insistent warble of the telephone.

Jancy looked at the phone with almost resentful
eyes, not really bothered whether to answer it or not.
But then she thought it might be Duncan, although
he was hardly likely to call at this time of day, and
she couldn't resist reaching out to pick it up. 'Hello?'

'Jancy?' It was Vicki's voice. 'Where on earth have
you been? I've been trying to get hold of you for
nearly two weeks.'

'Oh, hi. I've been away.'

'I gathered that.' Vicki sounded slightly exasperated. 'But where?'

'Oh—working.'

'But I rang the agency and they said you'd cancelled some work.'

'Yes, well—this was freelance work,' Jancy lied desperately.

'Really? Who for? It must have been a really good job if you're willing to break your contract with the agency to take it on,' Vicki commented on an intrigued note.

Knowing that Vicki wouldn't leave her alone until she found out who her mythical employer was, Jancy said, 'No, I didn't get paid at all. It was for charity.' Adding on a caustic note, 'Cancer research.'

'Oh, I see. I suppose you can afford to do that kind of thing occasionally now that you're going to marry Duncan,' Vicki remarked, but without any jealousy in her tone. She'd had plenty of offers from well-off men if all she'd wanted was to marry, but, like Jancy, she wanted to wait for the right man to come along. 'How is Duncan, by the way? Have you heard from him lately?'

'Yes, he's fine.'

'Great. Listen, are you doing anything for lunch tomorrow? We could meet and catch up on the gossip.'

'I'd like to, Vicki, but I feel as if I have a cold coming on. Maybe it would be better if we postponed meeting for a couple of days until I know for sure. I'd hate to give you a cold.'

As Vicki had some work coming up, she didn't want one either, so immediately agreed. 'OK, give me a call when you feel better. And keep in touch! I was beginning to get worried about you.'

She rang off, cutting Jancy off from the world that she had loved so much and worked so hard to reach. In a burst of anger and loneliness, Jancy got up and put on a cassette, turning the volume up so loud that she wasn't able to even think of anything else.

There was no fresh food to eat in the fridge, so that evening Jancy walked round to the nearest take-away for a Chinese. The hospital had given her a shaped lump of cotton wool in a cover to go inside her bra until the wound had completely healed. It didn't look too bad but felt completely unnatural because it had no weight. She felt lop-sided and was sure everyone would notice, so put on a loose overcoat even though the night was quite mild. And where she had walked tall and straight, with youth and vitality in her step, now she hunched forward and bent her left arm up over her chest, trying to hide what no one could possibly see.

When she got back to the mews she could hear the phone ringing in her flat, but she was clumsy trying to hold the take-away with her bad arm while she fumbled for her key, and it stopped before she could reach it. Darn! It was bound to have been Duncan and, as he was moving around, they had agreed that he would always contact her, so she didn't have a number to call him back. Usually Jancy liked Chinese food, but her appetite had gone and the food tasted like straw. Pushing the plate away, still almost full, she switched on the television, but it was the nine o'clock news and she was so low that all the bad news made her cry. Not that it took much at all to make her cry at the moment.

The phone rang again and she picked up the receiver with trembling fingers, but it was a woman's voice that said, 'Jancy?'

'Yes.'

'This is Margaret Lyle, Duncan's mother. My dear, we've been so worried about you. Duncan has been calling every night and not getting a reply. And for the past week I've been ringing, too. Has something happened to you?'

'Why, no. I've—I've been away. Working.'

'But didn't you let Duncan know? He's been going frantic.'

The thought of Duncan worrying about her brought fresh tears to Jancy's eyes, but she said, 'It was a last-minute thing; I just had to pack and go.'

'But Duncan insisted I call your agency and they said you weren't doing any work for them, that you'd cancelled some, in fact.'

'No, I—as a matter of fact I had a disagreement with them. I'm with another agency now,' Jancy told her, marvelling at how easy it was to lie. 'I'm so sorry you've had all this trouble. I would have phoned Duncan if I'd had a number to ring.'

'Yes, I'm sure you would.' But Mrs Lyle still sounded puzzled. 'But couldn't you have written to him at that post office address he gave you?'

'I suppose so, but I thought I'd be back before this—the weather was so bad and the shoot took much longer than expected,' Jancy prevaricated, adding soothingly, 'But I'm home now so I'll be able to explain to him myself.'

'Yes, of course. And he's given me a number where you can reach him if you phone tonight.' She gave Jancy the number, making sure that she'd got it right, then said, 'My dear, I'm coming up to London with Olivia next week to do some shopping. We shall be staying at Duncan's flat, and I thought it would be nice if we could all have dinner together; perhaps even go to a concert or something. It's so much easier to talk about the wedding when the men aren't around. Will that be all right?'

'Why, yes, of course,' Jancy said with difficulty. 'Just let me know when you're coming and what you want to see and I'll book some tickets. My treat,' she added firmly.

'Oh, but that really isn't necessary. We can——'

'No, I insist.'

'Well, that's most kind of you. Shall we say next Thursday, then? And there's a good concert on at the Barbican that night.'

'Fine. And I'll book a table somewhere.'

'And you will be sure to phone Duncan at once, won't you? He's been so worried.'

'Yes, I'll do it now. Sorry you've had so much trouble reaching me. See you next week, then. Love to everyone. Bye.'

She replaced the receiver, already hating herself for being a hypocrite. Because she knew there was no way she was going to be able to face Duncan's mother and sister, to be able to spend an evening with them trying to pretend that everything was OK. So it would put a time limit on her plans. Looking at the New Zealand number she'd been given, Jancy went to pick up the receiver again, but then changed her mind. She needed time to think of what she was going to say to Duncan.

After clearing up the remains of her meal, Jancy went into the bathroom to get ready for bed. She had lost weight—besides in the obvious way. The skin of her face clung to her cheekbones and there were dark shadows round her lack-lustre eyes. I look—lifeless, she thought. Like a zombie. The light dressing that covered the wound would need to be changed but she hadn't been able to bring herself to even look at it in the mirror yet. Tomorrow or the day after she'd go round to the hospital and get the nurse there to put on a fresh dressing. It was almost healed now, anyway. After a couple of days she probably wouldn't need a dressing, and then she could be fitted with a prosthesis—a nice, up-market word for a falsie; a long word to act as a false front for the emotional upheaval and despair of thousands of women.

Going into her bedroom, Jancy got into bed and propped herself up against the bedhead, trying to gather her courage to talk to Duncan. But the extension rang before she could lift the receiver. Slowly she reached out and picked it up.

'Jancy?' Duncan's voice came sharp and anxious across the miles.

'I know what you're going to say and I'm sorry,' she cut in before he could speak again. 'A rush job came up and there was no way I could let you know.'

'And you're all right?' The relief in his voice was plain to hear.

'Yes, fine—except for a cold.'

But Duncan hardly waited for her to finish before, his relief giving way to the natural reaction of anger, he said forcefully, 'You could easily have let me know if you'd tried, Jancy. You could have left a message with my parents or with the company. Didn't it occur to you that I'd be worried about you?'

'I've said I'm sorry. I didn't think I'd be away that long but——'

'I damn near got on a plane to come over there and find out what had happened to you! Have you no sense of responsibility?' His voice was sharp with too recent anxiety.

Consumed by guilt, the only way Jancy could stop herself from breaking down was to take refuge in angry defensiveness. 'For heaven's sake! I've said I'm sorry—what more do you want? I'm not used to being tied down and having to account for every second of my time!'

'Tied down!' Duncan's voice exploded with rage. 'My God, is that how you see it? We're engaged. I have a right to know when you decide to go away. And why didn't you call me back tonight after my mother gave you the number? She rang me herself to tell me she'd given it to you.'

'I was in the middle of having something to eat. I am allowed to finish my meal before I report to you, aren't I?'

'Don't be so damn ridiculous!'

'All right, I won't!' And Jancy slammed down the receiver. She sat there, chest heaving, bright flushes of colour on her pale cheeks. They had quarrelled and it had been all her fault. She had lied to him and made him hate her. And all because of this stinking, rotten operation. Putting her face in her hands, Jancy burst into heart-broken, tearing sobs of anguish.

The phone rang again within minutes and she knew that it was Duncan. It would be better if she didn't pick it up; a quarrel would suit her plans. But if she didn't answer he might carry out his threat and get on a plane. Wiping her eyes with a handkerchief, she reached out for the receiver.

'Jancy, I'm sorry.' He waited for her to speak but when she didn't said ruefully, 'Jancy? Are you crying? Oh, lord, I'm sorry, darling. I didn't mean to yell at you. I was so darn worried...'

'I—I know. I'm sorry, too.' A sob broke from her that she couldn't stifle.

'Please don't cry, darling. You make me feel like a monster.'

'No. It's—it's just that I'm very tired and I feel as if I've got a cold coming.'

'My poor love. I ought to be shot. I must let you get some rest. I'll call you tomorrow night.'

'Will you be at the same number? I'll call you if you like.'

'All right; then I won't disturb you if you decide to have an early night. Take care of yourself, my darling. And remember that I love you.'

'And I you. So much.' Her voice broke and Jancy had to grip the receiver hard. 'Goodnight, my love.'

'Jancy?' His voice troubled, it seemed for a moment as if Duncan would question her further, but then he said, 'Goodnight,' in return and she quickly put down the receiver.

The next day was a very busy one: Jancy went round to an estate agent's office and told him that she wanted to let her flat, furnished, for a period of two years. Reassured that she would have no trouble at all in finding a tenant, Jancy told him to make all the arrangements through her solicitor and to pay the rent directly into her bank. She then booked two tickets for the Barbican concert for Mrs Lyle and Olivia and reserved a table for them at the restaurant in the arts complex. Just doing those few things had made her feel deathly tired. They had told her at the hospital that, after such a major operation, she should rest for a few hours every day at first, but Jancy pushed herself into going to a local department store and buying lots of baggy sweaters and long, loose cardigans. After this week, she would have every hour of every day to rest.

Her phone call that night to Duncan was just like old times; he was especially loving, telling her how much he missed her and longed to be home. He was full of plans for the oast-house and for the wedding, asking her to decide on where she'd like to go for a honeymoon. 'We could go skiing,' he suggested eagerly. 'Or to Bali or the Bahamas if you'd prefer somewhere hot. Anywhere you like.'

'OK. I'll—I'll think about it,' she promised.

'And decide on a date. How about a Christmas wedding?'

Somehow she managed to laugh. 'Your mother would never forgive me. All those preparations as well as shopping for Christmas! I've arranged to go out with her and Olivia next week, by the way.'

Her ruse to distract him worked and they talked of other things until Duncan reluctantly said goodnight so that she could go and nurse her imaginary cold.

That night she felt fagged to death but couldn't sleep; it was impossible to lie on her left side and she had to rest her arm on a pillow, which felt so un-natural that she just couldn't get used to it. She had to drag herself out of bed in the morning. Another busy day: arranging for meters to be read and future bills to be sent to her solicitor; filling in forms at the post office so that her mail could be re-addressed. And in the afternoon she went to the hospital and had a prosthesis fitted. But she couldn't bring herself to wear it and carried it home in its box. She wanted to throw it on the floor and trample on it. Because it was an admission that now she had to live a lie, a pretence that she was whole. Wearing it denigrated her even further because it was a deceit, and a pun-ishment because her own body had betrayed her and in doing so had become a vile and ugly thing. Jancy was so upset that she knew there was no way she could talk to Duncan that night without telling him the truth; she just didn't have the strength. So she took the coward's way out and left the receiver off the hook.

The next morning Jancy packed. There wasn't a lot she wanted to take. Just her prints and some books; her cassette player and collection of music. Going through her wardrobe was hell. She had such beautiful clothes. But most of them were tight-fitting dresses and tops. None of which she would ever wear again. Or the gorgeous lace underwear in a whole range of colours. Now she was stuck with a passion-killer of a bra to take the falsie, which she couldn't wear anyway because she couldn't get her arm up high enough to fasten it. Ruthlessly, Jancy threw the underwear in the rubbish bag and bundled up the other things and took them to a second-time-around shop, telling the startled salesgirl to give the proceeds to charity, adding fiercely, 'And make sure it's cancer research.'

All her leisure clothes, and what loose-fitting stuff she had, she packed into suitcases, adding just the bare necessities of toiletries and make-up—and she even hesitated over adding the latter, but habit rather than anything else made her put some in. In the afternoon she began to spring clean the flat, but was overcome by exhaustion and dropped on the bed, immediately falling into a deep sleep.

When she woke it was night and the phone was ringing. She groped for it, saying a sleepy, 'Hello?'

'Darling?'

'Oh, hello, Duncan. What time is it?'

'Were you asleep? Sorry, sweetheart. How's the cold?'

'About the same, I suppose. You OK?'

'Yes, fine, except for wishing I were with you every hour that passes. What happened last night; I called but got the engaged signal every time?'

'Yes, sorry about that. I took the receiver off the extension in the bedroom while I was having a nap and forgot to put it back on again.' She paused. 'Duncan...' Jancy bit her lip, knowing that this was the last time she would ever speak to him and hardly able to bear it. 'I'm sorry, I took a pill and I feel so sleepy. Do you—do you mind if we leave this until tomorrow? Maybe I'll feel better then.'

'Yes, of course.' He was immediately full of remorse. 'I'm sorry to have woken you. Look, I'll give you this number and you can call me when you feel up to it.' He gave her the number and she repeated it but didn't write it down. 'Goodnight, then, my love.'

'Goodnight.'

'Jancy?'

'Yes?'

He was reluctant to let her go. 'Nothing. Just that I love and miss you.'

Slowly she put the phone down, the words still in her ears, in her mind. Where they would always be for as long as she lived.

Strangely, Jancy woke feeling better the next morning. Probably because everything was done and there was no going back. Last night she had finished cleaning the flat, and now took the key round to the estate agent's after packing all her belongings into her car. From the estate agent's she drove round to

Highgate and let herself into Duncan's place. Jancy stayed there longer than she'd intended because she went round everything again; touching his clothes, looking at the portraits, trying to wish herself back in time.

But that wasn't to be. Taking two letters from her bag, she propped them up on the mantelshelf. The first letter was to his mother and contained the tickets for the concert with a short note of apology that she wouldn't be able to join them. The second letter was addressed to Duncan and was very brief for the import of its contents. It read, 'Duncan. There's no easy way to say this. I've met someone else and I'm leaving London to go and live with him. I'm sorry, but it's just the way things happened. Jancy.' And, taking the rose diamond from her finger, she carefully put it back in its box and laid it beside the letter. Then, her heart breaking, she turned and ran out of the flat.

CHAPTER THREE

IT TOOK Jancy three days to reach the cottage in Yorkshire. After she left Highgate the first day she felt so sad and depressed that tears kept coming of their own accord and she could hardly see to drive, so she pulled off the road not long after she'd left London and booked into a motel. The receptionist there could hardly help but notice the state she was in and asked her if she was ill, but Jancy muttered something about a bereavement and hurried to her room. At first she felt guilty about telling another lie and couldn't think why she'd said it, but as she lay on the bed in the soulless room it gradually came to her that she *had* suffered a form of bereavement. She had lost Duncan. And she had lost the life that she knew. Everything, in fact. So surely there could be no greater bereavement than that?

The following day she pushed on up the motorway, finding it impossible to use the safety strap and her arm aching so much that she had to stop and rest several times, finally giving up to spend the night in a small guest-house near Sheffield. By the time she finally reached the cottage the next day she felt as if she'd been travelling for weeks.

Somehow Jancy had expected it to be raining, probably because she felt so depressed, but, as she drove through the succeedingly narrower lanes, the sun lay across the rolling hills of the moors like a warm caress, turning the heather to a rich Persian carpet of colour. She had to stop a couple of times and look up the way on a map. Her great-aunt had been kind to her when she was a child and she could vaguely remember going to the cottage to spend a few holidays after her parents had split up. But her aunt had only used the cottage in the summer months and that had been the time when Jancy had been shuttled from one parent to the other, depending on who won the fight to have her for the holidays. So she didn't really remember much about it.

Jancy stopped at a crossroads to consult the map again, then sat back, trying to recall her holidays here. Aunt Cecily had met her at the station in a really old car, she recalled, and they had often gone out in it to visit ancient seaside towns and spend the afternoon on the beach. Then there had been long walks over the moors and picnics by a small river that you crossed by stepping-stones. Dim recollections of ruined abbeys and hours spent in intriguing museums came into her mind. And when it rained they had sat round a big log fire and Aunt Cecily had taught her how to sew. She had started a sampler, she remembered, and had taken it home to finish, but without her aunt's enthusiasm to push her it had been put in a drawer and forgotten.

Turning left, Jancy drove up a steep hill, careful to watch out for the sheep that wandered on to the road from the unfenced moorland. A mile further on she went downhill again and passed through a small village that wasn't much more than a cluster of houses and which she didn't remember at all. Then a farm that looked vaguely familiar, and on for only a couple of hundred yards before drawing up beside the cottage. It was bigger than she remembered and yet somehow smaller, too. Double-fronted, it stood square and solid, sideways on to the road so that it looked out down the hill to the village she'd passed and the stream that threaded its way along the dip in the moor, the fast-flowing water coruscating in the sunlight. The roof of the cottage was slate, grown green with lichen, and the walls of grey limestone. The door and window frames had once been painted a bright green but now looked shabby and weather-beaten. The garden, too, was waist-high with weeds and flowers that had gone wild.

Slowly Jancy got out of the car and was immediately aware of the bite in the air and the fresh, clean smell that told her she was near the top of the moor. She tried to think how long ago it was that Aunt Cecily had died and realised with some dismay that it must have been nearly three years. And she hadn't done a thing about the house in all that time. She had always been meaning to come up, of course, but the time had gone by so quickly. But then it always does when you're happy, she thought wretchedly.

The gate stood open, sagging on its hinges. Nettles, and the thorns of an old rose bush caught at her trousered legs as she went up the path and round to the front door. The key turned in the lock all right but the door wouldn't open. She pushed at it in a sudden rage but it must have warped or something. There were a couple of other keys on the ring. Going round to the back, Jancy found that one fitted the back door which opened easily.

It was eerie walking round the cottage, still full of the furniture and belongings that her aunt had left. Jancy could almost hear Aunt Cecily's voice now, cheerfully calling her to get up because they were going on some outing. The place was very damp; there were great patches of it on the walls and the whole house smelt mouldy. Again wishing that she'd given some attention to the place, Jancy forced open a window to reveal a spider's larder of dead flies concealed round the frame. She drew back in distaste. She couldn't possibly stay here, not with the house in this state. Dismally, she wondered whether to put the cottage up for sale. She could always go and find a hotel for tonight. But she needed somewhere to live long term and her tired brain just couldn't cope with the problem of trying to find somewhere else. She found that the front door had been bolted from the inside. The bolts were stiff and difficult to undo with only one arm, but she managed it in the end and threw the door open to let in the sunlight.

The view down the valley was breathtaking. Jancy stood in the doorway, remembering it all over again. The sun was warm on her face and suddenly she felt better. If she sold the cottage she would only have to buy or rent another house, so she might as well stay here and try and make the best of it. The resolution made, Jancy went out to the car and drove it into the yard at the back where there was an old barn that Aunt Cecily had used as a garage. There was a padlock on the large double doors of the garage but, strangely, there were no weeds obstructing them. Jancy curiously tried the third key on the ring in the padlock and it sprang open with well-oiled ease, as did the garage doors. She pushed them wide, then gave a little gasp of pleasure; her aunt's old car, so well remembered, stood in the centre of the garage, its cream paintwork gleaming with polish, the chrome shining.

Going inside, Jancy walked round the car, her mind filled again with memories of old jaunts. When she'd been a child, it had just been an old car, but now she realised that it was old enough to be a veteran vehicle, a collector's item. It was a Daimler, she saw, and must have been worth quite a lot of money even when it was new. Glancing round the rest of the garage, Jancy saw that it was crowded with all the usual household rubbish and garden tools, all thick with dust and cobwebs. Her eyes swung back to the car, without a speck of dust on it. Someone must have been coming here to clean it. A feeling of unease ran through her and Jancy hurried out of the garage and locked it behind her. But out in the sunlight again she felt silly: perhaps her aunt had left instructions that the car was to be looked after.

The sitting-room, the right-hand front room, seemed to be the driest in the house. Jancy dumped everything she'd brought with her into it and then sat down on an old chaise-longue to rest. Ordinarily she would have set to work straight away to clean the place up but she had no energy left. She'd start tomorrow.

It was about an hour later that Jancy woke from a fitful doze. The sun had gone down and the air was much cooler. Shivering a little, she got up and went out into the hall to close the front door. It had grown darker too, so she flipped on the light switch. Nothing happened. The bulb must have gone, she realised, and went into the kitchen. But neither the light there nor any of the electrical gadgets would work. Of course, the electricity must have been turned off years ago. Experimentally she turned on the water taps but there wasn't even a gurgle. Darn! Why hadn't she thought of all this before she came up here? She could have phoned her aunt's solicitors and asked them to get everything turned on again before she arrived.

In the state she was in it would have been easy to have given way and burst into tears again, but Jancy gritted her teeth and told herself to look on it as a challenge. Candles, that was it. She remembered that they had once had a power cut when she'd been staying here and her aunt had put out lots of candles. It had seemed very romantic at the time because she had been given one in an old-fashioned holder to light her way to bed. They must be here somewhere. Eventually Jancy found a whole packet of candles in a built-in cupboard in the kitchen, along with the pretty ceramic holder. Luckily she'd brought some matches with her so she lit the lot, placing them round the sitting-room, dispelling the shadows.

Dusting off a small table, Jancy opened the pack of sandwiches she'd bought earlier that day and began to eat, mentally making a list of all the things she would have to do tomorrow. A faint sound from the back of the house made her suddenly tense. Then she relaxed. Mice, she supposed, if nothing worse. She ought to have been prepared for that. But she had been so caught up in getting away from London, and the agony of losing Duncan, that she hadn't given a thought to the conditions she would find here. Somehow she had expected it to be just the same as when Aunt Cecily had been here: warm and welcoming, a place of cheerful peace and happiness. But that was what Aunt Cecily had made it, so how could it possibly be the same without her? Jancy sighed and made a mental note to add mice poison to her shopping-list.

The door suddenly went crashing back on its hinges and a man burst into the room! He was burly and bearded and he carried a gun which he pointed straight at Jancy. She screamed in startled terror and sprang to her feet, knocking the table over. Her first thought was that he meant to rape her and she screamed again. Then: if he rapes me he'll see I've only got one breast. That thought was even worse than the fear of rape. Lunging towards the fireplace, Jancy grabbed the poker in her right hand and held it like a club. Her other arm went protectively across her chest. 'Get out of here!' she yelled in panic-stricken fear.

But the man seemed to be as taken aback as she was and was staring at her in amazement. But his voice was still threatening as he said roughly, 'What the hell do you think you're doing here?'

'Get out!' Her voice rising hysterically, Jancy cried, 'Get out, or I'll call the police.'

Lowering the barrel of the gun, the man said, much more mildly, 'I was about to say the same thing—only there isn't any phone.'

He took a step towards her but Jancy brandished the poker in terror. 'Don't you come near me.'

'All right. Look, I'm putting the gun down.' His voice was almost soothing now as he leaned the gun against the sideboard. 'Now, suppose you tell me what you're doing in Miss Bruce's cottage.'

'But I'm Miss . . .' Jancy stopped, realising that he must mean her aunt. And he spoke with a slight but noticeable Yorkshire accent so he must be a local man. 'I'm Jancy Bruce, Cecily's great-niece. Who are you?'

He gave a surprised grunt. 'So you've come to see the place at last. It's about time. My name's Linton, Robert Linton. I own the farm just down the road. I saw the light in here so I came to take a look. I thought a tramp or thieves might have broken in.'

'Oh. Oh, I see.' Jancy gratefully lowered her poker and looked at him more closely. The beard made him look older, but she thought that he must be between forty and forty-five. He was wearing boots and farming clothes: cord trousers and a padded jerkin over a check shirt. She ought to know him, she realised, and tried to visualise him without the beard and thirteen years or so younger—about Duncan's age. Dredging her memory she recalled a cheerful young man who had looked after the car and garden. Yes, and he had a wife who'd looked after the cottage while her aunt was away. And she seemed to recall a young baby, too. But the baby would be a teenager now.

He glanced at her luggage on the floor. 'Come up here for a holiday, have you?' he asked disparagingly.

'No, I've come to stay. I'm going to live here,' she added as much to confirm her own decision as to inform him.

Robert Linton's eyes went over her and his mouth twisted in amused disbelief, but then Jancy stepped forward into the light of the candles and he saw her pallor and the dark shadows around her eyes. He frowned, then nodded towards her arm where it was still bent protectively across her chest. 'Have you hurt yourself?'

She glanced down, only now realising what she was doing. 'Oh. Yes. I—I hurt my arm.' Adding quickly, 'I strained it.'

'And you intend to stay here, with the place in this state?'

'Yes. I've—I've nowhere else to go.'

He gazed at her, not understanding, but too much of a Yorkshireman to question her further. 'You'll need some water, then. I'll go and turn it on.'

He went out of the back door and lifted a manhole cover in the yard to turn the stopcock underneath. After a great deal of gurgling and rattling of pipes, water came shooting out into the kitchen sink.

'Oh, *thanks*,' Jancy said gratefully. 'You wouldn't know how to turn the electricity on as well, would you?'

'You'll have to get the electricity board to do that. But, if you like, I'll phone them first thing tomorrow and ask them to do it.'

'Please.' He had followed her back into the sitting-room. 'Is it you who comes to clean the car?'

He nodded. 'I wrote to you via your solicitor when your aunt died offering to buy the car and this house.'

'Did you?' Jancy frowned, vaguely remembering something of the sort, but she had been working in America at the time and had forgotten all about it.

'I'd still like to buy them from you. If you're hard up I can lend you some money on account——'

'I'm not hard up.'

'But you said you had nowhere else to go,' he reminded her with a frown.

'It doesn't necessarily follow that I have no money.'

'I see. I beg your pardon,' he said stiffly.

'No, I'm sorry.' Jancy lifted a tired hand to push her hair back from her face, trying to think. It was obvious that he was more interested in the car than in the house, or he would have kept that in good condition, too. 'I appreciate your offer but—look, could we talk about this tomorrow? It's been a long day, and your bursting in like that has completely thrown me.'

With another grunt, Linton picked up his gun. 'I'll bid you goodnight, then.'

When he'd gone Jancy made herself up a bed on the settee and lay down on it in a daze. After being scared out of her wits, she was now feeling extremely grateful that Mr Linton and his wife were nearby. She hadn't given the solitariness of the cottage much thought, but it was nice to know that he was on hand with his gun. Thinking that he would probably be good at dealing with rats and mice, too, she smiled a little. But then her thoughts filled with Duncan and for the third night running she cried herself to sleep.

The settee grew uncomfortable after a while and Jancy spent a restless night, getting up as soon as it was light to wash as best she could in cold water. Remembering that she would be seeing Mr Linton, she managed somehow to do up her bra and insert the prosthesis, doing it quickly so that she wouldn't have time to think about it, but still covering herself with a loose sweater and a long cardigan over that. Then she sat down to write out a list of all the things she needed to do that day. The priority was to get the cottage dry and clean, she decided. Her aunt had kept a store of logs and kindling at the back of the house; it took several journeys because she couldn't carry much at a time, but Jancy eventually laid the fire and put a match to it. Robert Linton banged on the back door and walked in just as she was coughing her way through the resulting cloud of smoke from the chimney.

'Might be an idea to have the chimney swept first,' he said, laughing, and raked out the fire.

'I'll add it to my list,' she said wryly, indicating the sheet of paper on the table.

'No need. There's a man in the village who'll do it for you.' He picked up her list. 'And I can use the phone to arrange for a lot of these things to be done. You'll need some oil too, for the central heating your aunt had put in.'

'That's very kind of you. Mr Linton, I've been thinking about the car.'

'Yes?' He gave her an eager look.

'I'd like you to have it. I don't know why my aunt didn't leave it to you. I didn't even know it was here, and it would be a pile of rust by now if you hadn't taken such good care of it.'

But even while she was still speaking he had begun to shake his head emphatically. 'I can't accept it. It's very kind of you, mind. And I appreciate it. But there's no way I can take it from a young lass like you.'

Jancy frowned, recognising a brick wall when she saw it. Then an idea came to her. 'In that case I'll sell it to you.'

'For how much? You must ask a fair price, now.'

She shook her head. 'Not for money. I'll sell it to you for your help to get this house in order again.'

'But that wouldn't be right.'

'Yes, it would. You work out a fair price for the car against the cost per hour of your help and let me know when you've worked it off.'

For a few moments he looked her over assessingly, seeing her afresh in the daylight, then his mouth widened with a grin of amusement and he nodded. 'All right, we'll do it that way.'

'And I seem to remember your wife looking after the house for my aunt; do you think she would be able to come and help me clean it up?'

'My wife is dead,' Linton answered flatly.

'Did she die of cancer?' Jancy asked sharply, her own dread instantly filling her mind.

He looked surprised. 'No, it was a boating accident; she and the boy were drowned.'

'Your son, too?' Jancy looked at him in horror. 'Oh, I'm so sorry. Was it—was it recently?'

He shook his head. 'No, a good many years ago now.' He became brisk again. 'But I can ask a woman from the village to come up and give you a hand until your arm's better.' He was about to say something else but there was the sound of a car outside and he glanced through the window. 'Here's the postman— I haven't seen him call here for a good long time.'

The red Royal Mail van drew up outside and Jancy went to collect the letters, surprised that there should be any until she remembered that it had taken her so long to get here. There were two letters: one direct from her solicitors, and one re-addressed by the Post Office. The latter bore a New Zealand stamp and was in Duncan's bold and distinctive handwriting. Jancy stared down at the envelope, for a few seconds thinking that it must be a letter of recrimination, but then realising that it was too soon—even if he knew she'd run away there wouldn't have been time for Duncan to write from New Zealand.

She became aware that Robert Linton was speaking to her. 'Sorry. What did you say?' Jancy turned towards him a face that had lost every vestige of colour.

Seeing her face and the way she was gripping the letter, he changed his mind. 'I'll do what I can with this list and let you know how I get on later.'

'Yes—thank you.' But he was hardly out of the door before Jancy was ripping open Duncan's letter.

It was a love-letter. Written after their row over the phone, it was full of apology and regret, of longing and love. Jancy could imagine Duncan putting down the phone and immediately sitting down to write what was in his heart. Every word was both joy and pain. To have him love her so and have to give him up was a cruel torment. Each word of love was like a twisted knife in the wound where her breast had been, but Jancy knew that she would keep and treasure this letter for the rest of her life.

It was a long time before she put the letter carefully away in her handbag and opened the other envelope. It contained a letter passed on from the estate agent saying that her flat had been let, and also enclosed a note from Vicki that had been pushed through the door. It demanded to know what had happened to her and for Jancy to get in touch. Guiltily, Jancy sat down at once to write to her friend, but merely said that she had gone away and not to worry about her. After some hesitation, Jancy decided not to put the address of the cottage but gave that of her solicitor instead. 'I'll be down in London from time to time,' she wrote, 'and I'll look you up then.'

In the afternoon Jancy went to the nearest town to shop and posted the letter there, then turned away to start her new life.

After three weeks of hard work the cottage was completely habitable again. The leaks were mended, the rooms dried out and redecorated, the mouldy bedding and carpets thrown out and replaced by new ones. Jancy had had a lot of help of course, from Robert Linton, whom she had come to call Rob as all the villagers did, from a small army of tradesmen, and from Anne Rudby, a kind and motherly woman who lived in the village in the valley, and who had the reputation of making the best Yorkshire pudding this side of the county.

The mail van had called a couple of times more, but one morning it brought another letter in Duncan's handwriting, sent on from her solicitor, but with an English stamp this time. Jancy looked at the envelope for a long time without opening it. It was postmarked only three days ago and she knew that he must have come back from New Zealand early and had read her farewell letter. So this, then, was the letter of recrimination that she had dreaded. It took great courage to open it. She didn't want to; she wanted the precious love-letter to be his last word, not this. She almost threw it on the fire, but couldn't, and after a while she slowly slit open the envelope.

Duncan's letter was as terse as hers had been. 'You owe me an explanation. If you don't have the courage to phone or call on me at my flat, then I shall be at the Bacchus wine bar between twelve-thirty and two every day until the fourteenth of November. Duncan.'

The Bacchus wine bar was close to Jancy's London flat and it had become their favourite place for a meal. She remembered how they had sat across the table from one another, lifting their glasses in a silent toast, the air magnetic with anticipation in the knowledge that soon they would go back to the flat and make love. A stirring of awareness and need deep inside her caught Jancy by surprise and made her angry; what right had this deformed body to want what it could never have again? She put the letter aside, telling herself to forget it, but the thought of Duncan waiting every day brought on a fresh bout of despair and longing. To see him again, just once—then it occurred to her that she would be in London later that week anyway, because she had an appointment to see her consultant.

Jancy fought the temptation every moment of every day and often long into the night. She fought it on the drive to the mainline station and on the whole of the train journey to London. Arriving the day before her appointment, Jancy stayed the night at a hotel near the station, and was glad that she'd arrived too late in the day for Duncan still to be waiting. At least the temptation could be put off till tomorrow. That evening she rang Vicki, but was lucky to find her at home as she was just leaving to go out on a date, so they arranged for Jancy to go round there for a meal the following evening.

Knowing that she was in the same city as Duncan, huge though it was, was enough to keep Jancy awake most of that night. The next morning she arrived at the hospital in plenty of time to see the consultant, who said that physically she was OK. However, he frowned over her thinness and wanted her to see a psychiatrist, but Jancy stubbornly shook her head.

On leaving the hospital Jancy caught a bus to Kensington, arriving there at about eleven forty-five. As she'd remembered, there was a fast food place almost opposite the wine bar. After only a short wait Jancy managed to get a seat by the window that gave her a good view of the wine bar, but where she couldn't be seen easily. The tray of burger and chips lay untasted in front of her as she waited tensely for Duncan to arrive at twelve-thirty.

He came early, striding along the street in a belted trench coat but bare-headed against the rain that had begun to fall. His face was tanned but looked thinner, his mouth drawn into harsh lines. As he walked along he looked around him, his eyes searching the crowds, and Jancy automatically drew back. At the door of the wine bar he paused for a moment, and she saw him brace his shoulders before walking in. Jancy looked down at the table, her emotions in turmoil, grateful to have seen him, but feeling deeply wretched inside for having caused his unhappiness. She thought that it would be the last she saw of him, but when she looked up she saw that Duncan, too, had taken a seat at a table in the window of the wine bar and was continuously looking out. So now she couldn't possibly leave until after he did.

The next hour and a half was unbearably long, and Jancy lost count of the number of times she had to fight off the impulse to run across to him and throw herself in his arms. She would have given anything to feel his love, his strength holding her. The place had filled up and Jancy had to share the table, the people giving strange looks at her untouched food and at her face as she brushed away tears.

'Are you all right?' A woman looked at her in unwilling concern and Jancy nodded and tried to smile.

Duncan gave her an extra quarter of an hour before he left the wine bar, his face taut and grim. He hailed a cab and when she was sure he was safely out of sight Jancy, too, took a taxi to her hotel where she locked herself in her room and gave way to grief, knowing that it had been a mistake to see him, that she had to try and put him out of her mind forever.

At seven that evening she forced herself to have a bath and change, and at eight took a taxi round to the block of flats where Vicki lived.

'Good grief! What's happened to you?' Vicki demanded as soon as she saw her. 'You look terrible.'

'Thanks.' Jancy took off the long cape she'd been wearing over the usual baggy sweater, and cord trousers tucked into knee-high boots. Her hair was pushed up under a wide-brimmed winter hat. But she'd tried to hide the fact that she'd been crying by putting on some make-up, and she was so tall and slender that she couldn't help but look classy.

Vicki gave her a frowning look. 'You've lost weight. And you look fagged to death. I take it that things haven't worked out with this man you ran away with?'

It was Jancy's turn to frown. 'I didn't say that I'd gone away with someone in my letter to you.'

'No, I know. Duncan told me.'

Jancy's eyes widened. 'Duncan? He came here?' She gave a frightened glance towards the door as if he might walk in at any minute.

'I'll say he did. Breathing fire and brimstone and demanding that I tell him where you were. And when I told him I didn't know he didn't believe me and got quite nasty. In the end I had to show him your letter before he would go away.'

Thanking her stars that she hadn't given Vicki her Yorkshire address, Jancy said, 'I'm sorry you had to go through that. It hadn't occurred to me that he would come here.'

'I just can't understand why you ditched him. You both seemed so in love. I thought yours was going to be one of those fairy-tale love-stories of all time that you only read about. Did something happen between you?' she asked curiously.

Jancy shook her head. 'No. I—I just couldn't go through with it, that's all. Don't let's talk about it. Tell me all that you've been doing. I want to hear all the gossip.'

'All right. But I've phoned through an order to the local Chinese take-away. I'll go out and get it and then we can talk while we eat.'

'Fine. Shall I come with you?'

'No, you stay here. You look so tired. I'll just get my coat.'

Vicki went to go to her bedroom but Jancy said, 'Here, take mine. And you'll need my hat; it's really cold outside.'

'OK, thanks. Pour yourself a drink.'

Vicki was longer than Jancy had expected and when she finally came in she quickly shut the door and put on the chain. 'My God, Jancy, you'll never guess what happened. Duncan was waiting for me when I came out of the Chinese.'

'What? But how?' Jancy stared at her in consternation.

'He grabbed hold of me and swung me round. He called me by your name.' Vicki dropped the carrier-bag with their meal in it on the table. 'Lord, I'm still shaking. His face was like thunder until he saw it was me. Then he looked completely stunned.'

Jancy had got quickly to her feet and caught Vicki's arm. 'But I don't understand. Why should he possibly think that you were me?'

'I worked it out on the way back,' Vicki answered, her voice high with excitement. 'Duncan must have had someone watching my flat. A private detective or something. And he must have recognised you when you arrived. Presumably he immediately got in touch with Duncan and when I went out wearing your coat and hat he followed me thinking I was you.'

Jancy stared at her appalled. 'And then when Duncan got there . . .'

'Exactly. He was ready to have the row of the century and was completely taken aback when he saw it was only me.'

'What happened then?' Jancy demanded tersely.

'I told him that he was mad and ran for home.'

They stared at each other for a few minutes, Jancy's eyes wide and frightened. 'He'll think the detective made a mistake,' she said hopefully.

'Possibly. But then again he might work it out and come up with the right answer.'

'He's hardly likely to think that you'd borrow my coat. After all, men never do that kind of thing.'

'No, but we used to swap clothes all the time, and he'd probably remember something like that. He could be outside now, waiting for you to leave.'

'Oh, no!' Jancy stared at Vicki in dread. 'I can't see him, Vicki, I just can't.'

'All right. Don't worry. We'll think of something.' She looked down at their take-away. 'We might as well——'

The sound of the front doorbell broke into her words. They stared at each other, round-eyed with horror, until Vicki said, 'I'll have to answer it or else he'll guess.'

Jancy nodded, but said in a frightened whisper, 'He can't know for sure. Try and convince him that he's made a mistake. And for heaven's sake don't let him in.'

'I may have to. Look, go outside on the fire escape until I get rid of him. Don't forget your bag.'

Jancy stood outside in the darkness, pressed against the wall. Then she heard Duncan's voice and knew that he had pushed his way in. Lights went on in Vicki's bedroom and the bathroom, then she heard Vicki say in an exasperated voice, 'Are you satisfied now? You've got a damn cheek, Duncan, forcing your way in here like this. I told you: I haven't seen Jancy for weeks. Now, would you please go, because I'm expecting friends?' Duncan didn't answer but went into the kitchen. As quietly as she could, Jancy climbed a couple of floors up the iron stairway and hid in the deeply shadowed angle of the wall, knowing that Duncan wouldn't overlook something as obvious as the fire escape. And just a few moments later she heard a window open below her as he must have looked out.

The window closed, slowly, reluctantly, but a couple of minutes later Vicki came out and gave a low call. 'It's all right, he's gone.'

Jancy came quickly down and Vicki locked the window behind her. 'You must be frozen.'

Jancy had been so tense that she hadn't even felt the cold, but she drank down the brandy that Vicki poured for her in one swallow. When she looked round Vicki was on the phone. 'Who are you calling?'

'Some of the girls. Duncan's bound to be still suspicious and watching for you, so we'll confuse him by numbers.'

Four of their modelling friends duly arrived, indignant that Jancy was being besieged by an

unwanted admirer and glad to help. They stayed for
a couple of hours, making a party of it, and creating
such confusion when they left by going out of the
main entrance, coming back again, and changing
clothes, that Jancy, wearing one of Vicki's coats and
a blonde hairpiece, was smuggled out quite easily.

That Duncan had come so close to finding her, and
so easily, gave Jancy a terrible fright. When she got
back to her hotel she tried to work it out and realised
that in her letter to Vicki—the letter that Duncan had
read—she'd said that she would look Vicki up the next
time she was in town. So Duncan must have set
someone to watch for her there. He must be desperate
to find her if he had gone to those lengths. She could
understand him wanting an explanation and waiting
at the wine bar for her to come, but to set someone
to watch Vicki . . . But was it out of love, or fury at
her betrayal?

She couldn't wait to leave London but had made
an appointment to see her solicitor the next morning
to sign some papers to do with letting the flat. It had
stopped raining and the sun was shining, but there
was a strong breeze that brought a definite nip of
winter to the air. Jancy took a taxi to the office block
in which the solicitors took up a whole floor and
hurried in, pulling her cape around her. There was a
receptionist on duty in the entrance hall who looked
at her in keen enquiry, but Jancy merely murmured
the name of the solicitors and took the lift up to the
second floor. Here she refused the offer of a cup of
coffee, explaining that she had a train to catch, and
so was dealt with quickly, leaving after only about
twenty minutes.

Emerging on the sunlit pavement, Jancy walked to the kerb and looked round for a cruising taxi. She waited for a few minutes without any luck, then started to walk towards the road junction in the hope of finding one in the busier street. But as she did so a cab came along and pulled into the kerb just outside the office block to drop a fare. Quickly she turned back and hurried towards it, waving her hand at the driver to let him know that she wanted to hire him. A man got hurriedly out of the taxi, looking at the office block before he glanced towards her—and then they both froze as Jancy looked straight into Duncan's furious eyes!

CHAPTER FOUR

'JANCY!'

For a few stunned seconds she stood transfixed, but Duncan's yell galvanised her into movement and she turned to run.

'Wait!' Duncan started to run after her but he hadn't paid the taxi and the cabby began to yell at him. Cursing, he had to turn back to throw a note at the driver, but the few seconds had given Jancy time to run down the road and leap on to the platform of a bus that was just pulling away from a stop.

The conductor saw her and grabbed her left arm to stop her falling off again, making her gasp with pain. 'You want to be careful what you're doing,' he grumbled at her.

'Sorry. Thanks.' Hurriedly looking back, Jancy saw that Duncan had run back to the taxi, pushing someone else out of the way to get back in and gesturing at the driver to follow the bus. Oh, hell! Now what was she going to do? When the bus got to the next stop Duncan could easily jump out and board it.

But the traffic was thick and the bus went through the traffic-lights at the junction just before they turned to red and the taxi was left behind to wait for the next change. Giving a gasp of relief at this temporary reprieve, Jancy found some money for the conductor and said, 'Please? Where is the bus going?'

He rolled his eyes in exasperation at her stupidity. 'Harrods and Hyde Park Corner,' he told her in exaggerated patience.

Realising that it wouldn't take long for the taxi to catch them up, Jancy knew she had to act quickly. The bus swung along at a fair pace without anyone wanting to get off for quite a way. Still standing on the platform, Jancy looked anxiously out of the back window. There were lots of black London taxis mixed up in the traffic but she thought she saw one in the distance that was overtaking wherever possible and gradually catching them up. Some other people moved on to the platform, ready to get out at Harrods. Jancy hid herself among them and, as soon as the bus drew into the kerb, before it had even stopped, she had jumped off and run into the huge department store, swinging through the heavy glass doors and pushing her way through the crowd of shoppers. But instead of going on into the store, she turned left and ran through it to another entrance just near the Tube station. After a frightened glance round, she fled across the road and down into the bowels of the Underground, hiding herself among the throng of people on the platform until a train pulled in a few agonisingly long minutes later. As she cowered in a seat, it seemed as if it would take forever for the doors to shut, but they did so at last. But it was only after she had travelled on for several stops that Jancy was able to relax the tension that held her in rigid apprehension and hopefully believe that she had lost Duncan at last.

Feeling like a fugitive, Jancy travelled home from a different station because a train went from there earlier, although it took a roundabout route and arrived later than the express. But she didn't care how long it took; she was just glad to sit back and close her eyes, thankful for every mile that took her away from London. It had been a mistake to go there. But how could she possibly have foreseen that Duncan would have set someone to watch for her at Vicki's flat—and presumably at the solicitor's, too—how else would he have arrived so opportunely? Jancy shivered, remembering the fierceness in his eyes. There was no way he would have let her go without demanding the truth, and she would have told him anything rather than that. She didn't care if he thought her cruel and immoral; it was far better for him to hate her than to feel guilty because he could no longer love or bear to look at the ugly thing that she had become.

She dozed on the train, tired out by all the trauma of the last few days, and was infinitely grateful to reach the cottage close on midnight. Going from room to room, Jancy switched on the lights and drew the curtains against the cold and the dark. The central heating was on and there was a smell of new paint and carpets, of beeswax polish and pot-pourri, making the place warm and welcoming. Kneeling down, she put a match to the fire and sat back on the rug to watch the flames. So much had happened in the last few days. Leaning back against a chair, Jancy let her mind go back over it all, but always coming back to that moment when she had come face to face with Duncan and seen the fierce anger in his eyes. She had deliberately tried to make him angry so that he wouldn't be hurt and would forget her all the sooner, but she saw now that he wasn't the kind of man who would forgive and forget easily. She shivered, despite the warmth of the fire, and wondered how long it would be before he finally gave up.

The winter was a long one, high on the moors, with snow setting in early in January and lasting nearly till March. For Jancy it was a period almost of hibernation. Once a month she went to the nearest town to shop, buying not only food but books and tapes. She had begun sewing again, first by mending pieces that her aunt had done, and then to amuse herself during the long evenings. Her bread she made herself in the oil-fired Aga in the kitchen, but occasionally Jancy walked through the snow to the tiny shop in the village to buy fresh milk and vegetables. Rob Linton and Mrs Rudby were the only people she saw with any regularity. At Christmas Mrs Rudby had good-naturedly insisted that Jancy join her family for the day, her strong feelings of hospitality affronted at the thought of a young girl like Jancy being on her own. Rob Linton was also invited; it seemed that he went there every Christmas, like it or not, because he, too, was on his own.

Rather to her surprise, Jancy enjoyed the day; it would have been impossible not to with Mrs Rudby's natural good humour and determination not to leave them to themselves for a minute. Jancy had expected to stick out like a sore thumb, but Anne Rudby had a large and boisterous family who insisted that she and Rob join in all their games, finishing with an old-fashioned wassail bowl of hot punch, and carols sung round the Christmas tree.

Afterwards Rob walked her home up the hill, their hands deep in their pockets and scarves round their necks to keep out the cold. When they reached the cottage he lifted his head like an animal scenting the wind. 'There'll be snow soon.'

'Will you come in for a coffee?'

He shook his head. 'No, thanks.' But he seemed in no hurry to go. Looking at her, he said, 'You enjoyed today?'

'Yes. It was fun.'

'You need to get out and about more. You're too young to shut yourself away like you do.' Jancy couldn't think of anything to say, and Rob said in sudden intensity, 'I could hit the man who hurt you.'

Jancy gave him a startled look, as surprised by his fierceness as by his mistaken conclusion. 'It wasn't a man,' she said quickly.

But he didn't believe her. 'What else could it have been to drive you up here and leave you in the state you were in? I've never seen anyone so unhappy and broken-hearted.' She didn't answer, not wanting his pity, and he said roughly, 'Was it your husband? Are you married?'

'No.'

The surprise in her voice convinced him, and Rob nodded. 'All right, I don't mean to pry. Perhaps it's better forgotten. And your enjoying tonight proves that you're getting over it.'

He left her after seeing her safely into the house and when Jancy lay in bed that night she wondered if she was in fact getting over it. Physically over the operation, perhaps, but not over Duncan. She missed him every day, often stopping what she was doing to stand gazing into space, wondering if he had given up on her yet; where he was, what he was doing. Whether he had met someone else. But the nights were the worst, as she lay in bed, her body aching with frustration, longing for the lovingly remembered closeness of his body, of his touch, and the way he had groaned out endearments as he had lifted them both to the heights of rapture.

Those winter months gave Jancy the rest she needed, and they gave her time, too, to come to terms with her illness. As much as she ever could, anyway. She still couldn't bring herself to look at her reflection in the mirror and during the day covered herself as usual with layers of sweaters. Her arm was OK as long as she didn't overdo things, and she didn't get tired so easily any more. Her main enemy was loneliness. There was a pub in the village, but the unwritten moral code of the moors still frowned on women who went into pubs alone. Rob had taken her in there a few times, usually at lunchtime, but they had received so many speculative looks that Jancy had grown uncomfortable. This same moral code, although it allowed Rob to work at her house when she was alone there, wouldn't allow him to stay on and spend the evening with her.

At first this archaic attitude had annoyed Jancy, but she realised that if she wanted to grow into the way of life of the village then she must accept their standards. So she gradually became a little more self-sufficient and tried to be content with what she had. There was an old sampler, worked by a nine-year-old Victorian child, on the wall in the sitting-room. To pass the time, Jancy tried to copy it but gradually became ever more absorbed as she realised how intricate the design and how varied the stitches were. When she'd finished she realised how much enjoyment she'd got from the work and immediately started to design another. It gave her the idea that perhaps other women might be interested, and she might be able to make up sampler kits and sell them.

Jancy felt the first stirring of enthusiasm for anything since she'd had her operation. The feeling took her by surprise; she had thought that she wouldn't care about anything any more, that she would be completely numb for the rest of her life. Having arranged to see a consultant in York in future, she went there in February and spent the rest of the day browsing round the craft and needlework shops, seeing what kits they had on offer and becoming keener every minute on her idea for a cottage industry. At one shop she even spoke to the owner about it and the woman promised to look at the kits if she brought some along.

Filled with enthusiasm, Jancy went home and spent the next few weeks developing her idea, hardly noticing that the winter had melted away with the snow and spring was in the air. There were lambs out on the moor, black-faced and trying to run on spindly black legs, the air noisy with their bleating as they constantly called for their mothers. The moors lost their sodden look as new grass began to grow and flowers pushed up their bright heads. Jancy looked out at this annual renewal with wry, envious eyes, wishing that life could be as simple as nature. She didn't want the spring, her heart was still too heavy for it. It only made her more frustrated and lonely.

Going to her door one morning, Jancy saw Rob walking up the hill with his long, steady farmer's stride. He looked different, and she realised that he had left off his thick winter overcoat. He had shaved off his beard, too, but that had gone only a few weeks after she'd arrived. He looked much younger without it, and she had unthinkingly told him so, which had pleased him. He had done a great deal of work on the cottage and came up almost every day to see if she needed any jobs done. Jancy didn't want to take advantage of his kindness and kept asking him when the car would be paid for, until he had rounded on her and bluntly told her to shut up about it and he would let her know. But she knew he wouldn't. Jancy wasn't so wrapped up in her own misfortune that she couldn't recognise that Rob fancied her. It troubled her, but he didn't say anything, and she knew that he still believed that she was recovering from an unhappy affair. Then there was the twenty-year age gap between them which would also, she hoped, hold him back.

Coming up to the gate, Rob said, 'Have you made up your mind what you want done with the garden?'

Jancy shook her head. 'I haven't given it a thought.'

He made her put on her anorak and come outside and look at the overgrown mass of grass and trees. 'Your aunt made this into a nice garden and you ought to keep it up.'

'Maybe I'll grow some vegetables in that sheltered corner,' she offered.

Rob stood in the middle of what had once been the lawn, his hands on his hips as he looked round. 'I'll bring a scythe up here this afternoon and make a start. And in the meantime you can make a plan of the garden and decide how you want it.'

'I know nothing about gardening,' she protested.

'Then now's your chance to learn. I'll bring you up a couple of books to study. And when you've made up your mind we'll take my van and go over to the garden centre for some plants.'

'Ah, a designer garden.'

Jancy's voice had been teasing but Rob didn't get it; but then, they were often not on the same wavelength, although they got on well enough about basic, practical things.

They discussed the garden for a while longer; Rob telling her how Aunt Cecily had laid out the lawn and flower-beds. They walked round to the back of the house and Jancy noticed some people out on the moor. 'Look.' She pointed them out to Rob.

Shading his eyes to see against the low sunlight, he said, 'They're probably hikers. We get a lot of them up here, mostly from Easter onwards. They're always knocking on the door to ask if they can put a tent up in my fields, or have bed and breakfast. Your aunt sometimes used to take people in so don't be surprised if they knock on your door, too. But don't let them stay,' he warned.

Jancy gave him an amused look. 'It might be nice to have some company.'

'If you want some company then invite a friend to stay,' he said shortly, then saw by her face that she was teasing him, and grinned. 'Haven't you got any friends—girlfriends, that is?'

'Yes, of course.'

When he'd gone she thought about his suggestion. It *would* be nice to have some female company, but would any of her friends want to travel all the way up to Yorkshire to a place where there was no entertainment and where it would probably rain the whole time so that they couldn't even go out for a walk? Vicki might, for her sake, but Jancy couldn't see any of her other friends wanting to. It would be fun, though, to hear all the gossip of the model world, she thought wistfully. Going inside, Jancy found a notepad and sat down to write to Vicki, but then hesitated, realising that although she had only been away from London for a few months, she must be terribly out of touch. They had exchanged letters in those months of course—at least Jancy had written letters while Vicki had sent only a couple of hurriedly scrawled postcards from places where she'd been working, forwarded on by the solicitor. But then Jancy thought, What the hell, she can always say no.

So she sent off the invitation to come and stay at Easter, and after some deliberation gave the address of the cottage. Duncan was hardly likely to demand it of Vicki now; after all this time he must have come close to forgetting he had ever been engaged to her. The thought made Jancy feel sad, but she determinedly pushed it out of her mind. She must concentrate on her new lifestyle and just be thankful that the cancer hadn't yet recurred; that was all that mattered.

Rob came up the next day and they started work on the garden, Jancy helping now that her 'sprained arm' had healed. As the weather grew warmer more walkers appeared on the moor and tourists in cars often drove up to see the village because it was so old. But the tourists seldom came up the lane past the cottage unless they actually got out of their vehicles and took a walk. A couple of times hikers knocked and asked if she did bed and breakfast, but Jancy gave them a firm no.

'You ought to have a dog,' Rob said when she told him. 'I don't like to think of you up here by yourself.' And he gave a worried frown.

'Aunt Cecily lived up here by herself for years,' Jancy pointed out.

'That was different. She was elderly, while you ...
Well, you're young—and attractive.'

He gave her a searching look as he said it, but Jancy
turned away, thinking, If you only knew! Rob stood
up abruptly, his face withdrawn, and said he'd got to
go. Jancy looked at him in surprise but it wasn't until
some time later that she realised this was the first time
Rob had got near to paying her a compliment and she
had turned her back on him. She sighed, not wanting
to offend him, but afterwards thought that maybe it
was for the best—she certainly didn't want to give him
any kind of encouragement or foster vain hopes.

Vicki wrote and said she would come at Easter. 'I
could do with the rest. I'm completely worn out. But
I warn you: I shall probably sleep the whole time.'

In much excitement, Jancy went out to buy
furniture for the spare bedroom, and ordered new
curtains and matching sheets and duvet cover. The
furniture was due to arrive a few days later and Jancy
kept going to the door to look down the lane towards
the village to see if she could see the van. Once a flash
of light caught her eye and she looked across to the
far side of the moor to see the distant figure of a man
looking through binoculars. Probably a bird-watcher,
she surmised and dismissed it from her mind. The
furniture van arrived shortly afterwards and Rob came
to help carry it upstairs and put the bed together and
hang the curtain rail. While he was doing so a loud
knock sounded at the front door.

'It's probably some more hikers,' Rob advised her.
'Tell them to go down to Anne Rudby's; her sons are
away and she has a room to spare.'

'OK.' Jancy ran downstairs, eager to get back and
put the new curtains up. Pulling open the door, she

started to say, 'I'm sorry, I haven't any room, but if——' And then stopped dead. *'Duncan!'*

Jancy stood in paralysed stupefaction, all senses except sight deserting her as she stood in the doorway and stared at him. Her brain wouldn't work, nothing worked, until his eyes left her face and went swiftly over her figure in jeans and sleeveless waistcoat over a thick sweater. Then Jancy's left arm instinctively came up across her chest in the old protective gesture.

'Hello, Jancy. Long time no see.'

There was no triumph in his tone, only a world of bitterness. She couldn't speak and took an instinctive pace backwards, away from the menace in his eyes. But Duncan immediately stepped forward as if he thought she might shut the door in his face.

'Oh, no, you don't! I want to have a nice, long chat with you.' And he pushed past her into the house.

Jancy swayed against the wall, still bemused by surprise. 'How did you—how did you find me?' she asked on a faint, unsteady note.

Duncan's eyes flicked over her derisively. He didn't explain, merely said, 'Oh, it was inevitable that I would find you.'

Pushing open the door of the sitting-room, he went inside. Somehow Jancy managed to follow him.

He looked round scornfully. 'Is this the best he could give you—this man you ran away with?'

'It isn't—there wasn't—I mean it's mine,' Jancy floundered, in her stunned state hardly remembering she'd told him that she'd gone to be with another man.

'Where is he? Is he here?' Duncan demanded belligerently.

'No. I'm—I'm alone.'

'So it didn't work out. Serve you damn well right!'

'Why—why have you come? I don't——'

But Duncan was hardly listening. Reaching out he caught hold of her left wrist where it lay across her chest and dragged it down, looking at her fingers. 'Did he marry you?'

Instinctively Jancy cried out, afraid that he would brush her chest and realise it was false. 'Don't touch me!'

He stared at her. 'Why, you little slut!' Suddenly the violent, primitive emotions that he'd held under such tenuous control erupted to the surface and Duncan dragged her towards him. 'You owe me, you slut. You beautiful, cheating bitch!'

Jancy screamed again and tried to fight him off, slapping at him with her right arm. But Duncan jerked her against him and held her there, twisting her arm behind her, laughing cruelly as he put a hand under her chin and forced her head back. 'Now,' he said thickly. 'At last I can——'

The door crashed back as Rob erupted into the room. He tore her from Duncan's startled hold and Jancy went spinning, falling over a chair to end up on the floor. Taken by surprise, Duncan was unable to defend himself against a punch from Rob's hammerlike fist and he reeled back, but fury came to his aid and he gave a grin of devilish enjoyment as he sprang back and faced up to Rob, his fists clenched. 'So you *are* here. Come on, then. I've been waiting for this, you swine!'

'No! No, wait!'

But Jancy's cry went unheeded as Duncan swung a punch at Rob's head. Everything got very messy then. A low table went flying, the ornaments on it crushed under their feet, earth from a pot plant ground into the carpet. At first it was an even fight, because Rob was fitter and stronger, but Duncan was the younger and taller of the two, and had months of pent-up anger and frustration in his fists. Gradually he began to win, bearing down on poor Rob and driving him back.

'Stop it! Stop it, do you hear me?' But they took no notice of Jancy's yells. Desperately she caught hold of Duncan's arm and tried to pull him away, but he shook her off like an annoying insect and she ended up on the floor again. Then Rob went staggering back from a punch that almost knocked him out. Picking herself up, Jancy ran forward and threw herself in front of Rob, putting her arms round him and using her body as a shield. 'Leave him alone!' she yelled at Duncan over her shoulder.

He drew back in disgust, his breathing ragged and hair dishevelled, blood coming from a cut on his lip. 'All right, if he wants to hide behind a woman,' he sneered.

'Get out of the way! Let me get at him.'

Rob tried to push her aside but Jancy held him down. 'No! It's all right; I know him.'

He stared at her, one eye already beginning to swell. 'But he was attacking you. You screamed.'

'Yes, I know—but it wasn't what you think. Oh, Rob, you've been terribly brave, but please don't fight any more.'

He got to his feet, waving her away when she tried to help him. He staggered a little and put a hand up to his eye. 'Who is he, then?'

'More to the point—who the hell are you?' Duncan came forward antagonistically, still wanting to fight.

Jancy swung round on him furiously. 'You keep away! Rob is my neighbour.'

'You expect me to believe that?'

'It's true!'

'Then what was he doing upstairs—apart from the obvious?' Duncan sneered maliciously.

She glowered at him. 'He only came here to put up a curtain rail!'

Duncan looked completely taken aback and slowly lowered his fists. Jancy began to hope that she could keep them apart but Rob went and spoilt it all by saying fiercely, 'Is this the bastard you ran away from?'

'Well, well; it seems he's quite a close neighbour,' Duncan said with heavy sarcasm. Unable to stop himself, he caught hold of her arm. 'Well, aren't you going to answer him? Am *I* the bastard you've told him you ran away from—or was it the other man?'

'You take your filthy hands off her.' Having recovered a little, Rob was more than willing to start the fight again.

Realising that she had to split the two of them up, Jancy turned to Rob and said, 'Thank you for coming to help me, Rob, but please go now and let me handle this. I'll be all right.'

'I'm not going to leave you with him!' he protested explosively.

'He won't hurt me.'

'No? Then what the hell was he trying to do when I came in?'

Jancy flushed, making Rob's eyebrows rise as he realised, but it only increased his affronted anger, and Duncan didn't help by saying curtly, 'Mind your own damn business.'

'You filthy bastard! Don't you dare touch Jancy.'

Duncan smiled with smooth malice. 'Why not? It wouldn't be the first time—and I've done a hell of a lot more than touch her.'

'Why, you——'

Rob went to launch himself at Duncan again but Jancy suddenly lost her temper. 'All right!' she yelled at them. 'Go on, punch each other senseless. You're both stupid fools!' And she turned on her heel and marched out of the house.

They followed her almost immediately. Rob was still furious and would have gamely turned on Duncan if she'd given the word, but her anger had made him uncertain now. Duncan was quite plainly enjoying the situation. Coming up to her, Rob looked into her face and said, 'Is he telling the truth? Were you and he...?' He broke off, unable to put it into words.

'Yes,' Jancy answered baldly.

He stiffened, and Jancy sadly knew that she had lost a friend. 'I'll leave you to deal with him, then.' But he added coldly, 'I'll be at the farm. If you need me, yell. I'll hear you.'

She nodded gratefully. 'All right. Thank you, Rob.'

He strode off down the lane and Jancy watched him go. The sun was shining across the empty moor and birds were singing in the tree near the house where they were building their nest. It was all very peaceful and seemed a world away from the dark, menacing presence behind her who had already brought violence into her home in just the short time he had been there. A home that was no longer a safe haven. Slowly, Jancy turned to face him.

Duncan was waiting, a sardonically mocking look in his eyes.

'Why have you come here?' she said unsteadily, her courage fading.

'You know darn well why. Our relationship demanded a better explanation than just the few lines you left me with. I want to know who—and why.'

Turning away, Jancy crossed her arms over her chest, rubbing her shoulders as if she were cold. 'There's nothing here for you, Duncan. Not revenge. Not anything. Just forget we ever met, and go.'

'Oh, no.' He came and turned her round to face him. Looking at her intently, he said, 'I'm not going to give up that easily. When I read that charming little note you left I made up my mind that I'd find you— and that I'd make you pay for what you did to me.' She dropped her eyes before his and he said in disgusted tones, 'You little coward. Couldn't you even find the decency to tell me to my face?'

'Not every one is as—as strong as you, Duncan.'

'I thought you were.'

'Well, you were wrong; I'm not.'

'So I found out—the hard way.'

The roughness in his voice brought her eyes up to his face and her heart contracted. So much had happened since he'd arrived that Jancy hadn't really looked at him, but now she saw that his face was thinner, and there were grim lines around his mouth that hadn't been there before. Had she caused those? She wanted to lift her hand and touch the lines, to wipe them away. To kiss his mouth and make him smile again. A great surge of longing filled her and made her tremble.

Duncan's eyes widened and he frowned. 'Jancy?'

'I'm cold,' she said abruptly. 'I'm going in.'

He followed her into the sitting-room, the centre of her hideaway, that now looked like a Western bar-room after a brawl. Desperately needing something to do, Jancy set the table and chair back on their feet and began to pick up the broken ornaments.

'Leave that.' She ignored him, but Duncan repeated forcibly, 'I said leave that,' and pulled her to her feet.

'Don't you dare order me about! This is my home and you have no right to come here and wreck it,' she said fiercely.

Immediately his anger flared. 'I have every damn right! We were engaged to be married once, remember? You promised to become my wife.'

'Well, I changed my mind!' She went to walk past him to the kitchen but he caught her by the left shoulder, which was still tender from the operation. Jancy gave a cry of pain and dropped the pieces of china.

'What is it?' Quickly he let her go.

'I—I must have hurt my shoulder when I fell down,' she lied. She stood still, not looking at him, and he slowly raised his hand and touched her hair. A quiver ran through her and she said, '*Please*. Please go away, Duncan.'

His hand tightened convulsively. 'No!' he said harshly. 'I have to know why.'

'It wasn't anything you did,' Jancy said urgently. 'It was me. It was my fault.'

'Who was he?'

'No one you know. No one who matters.'

'Where is he now?'

She hesitated, searching for the right lie to tell. 'It didn't work out, so I came here.'

'Why didn't it work out?'

It was impossible to find an answer to that so Jancy took refuge in anger. 'Mind your own business!'

Still holding her hair, he jerked her towards him. 'It *is* my business. Why the hell else do you think I'm here?'

'Well, I'm not going to tell you anything more, so you can just go away.' Pulling herself free of his hold, Jancy stepped away from him. Taking a deep breath, she said with as much cold disdain as she could manage, 'You're just making a ridiculous fool of yourself. I got tired of you and went with another man, that's all there is to it. Why the hell you're making all this fuss about it, I don't know. It happens all the time.'

'Not to me it doesn't,' Duncan retorted vehemently. 'You're the only woman I've ever asked to marry me and I *know* that we had something good going for us. I want to know just why you threw all that away—and I'm going to stay here until I find out.'

Jancy stared at him, helpless in the face of his determination. 'But—but you can't.'

'Too bad.'

'But I don't want you here,' she burst out.

Duncan had started to turn away, but at that he swung round to face her again, a look of such bleak anger in his eyes that Jancy drew back in sudden fear. 'I ought to knock your head off,' he said savagely.

'You already tried that with Rob and it didn't solve anything.'

'No, but it made me *feel* a hell of a lot better,' Duncan retorted, his fists slowly unclenching.

He turned away and Jancy went out to the kitchen to fetch a dustpan and brush. He didn't help her to clean up the mess, just leaned against the wall by the door and watched her, a grim look on his face. When she'd done, Jancy came back into the room and sat down in a chair, reaction starting to set in and her legs unsteady.

Looking across at her, Duncan said shortly, 'I meant it; I'm not leaving here until I've got all the answers I want.'

She shook her head. Then, not wanting to antagonise him further, said, 'How did you find me?'

Crossing to sit on the deep window-seat, Duncan gave a mocking laugh. 'I suppose you thought you'd completely covered your tracks. But I came close to catching you that time in London.'

'You came close twice—I was in Vicki's flat when you came there.'

His head came up at that. 'You couldn't have been. I searched the place thoroughly.'

'I was out on the fire escape, but I climbed higher.'

'Clever.' He looked at her moodily. 'When I scared you off at your solicitors I knew you wouldn't go back there, so I tried your agency and all your friends I could think of, but you seemed to have just disappeared. No one knew where you were—or if they did they weren't telling. For weeks I got nowhere. Then I remembered your saying that you'd inherited a cottage in Yorkshire from an aunt. And the letter you sent to Vicki also had a Yorkshire postmark, so I hired people to go through the phone books for everyone named Bruce in the county.' He smiled wryly. 'But of course you're not on the phone. So then I got them to go through all the electoral rolls. Do you know how many people there are named Bruce in Yorkshire? Remind me to give you the figures some time.

'Eventually they narrowed it down to women who owned property in more remote areas—I'd remembered that you'd said the cottage was miles away from anywhere—and I came up here myself to go through the last short list of names.' He paused, and Jancy tried not to imagine the anger that had driven him on. But as if guessing her thoughts, Duncan said, 'I was very determined to find you, you see.' He went on, 'I wasn't sure that this was the right place or that you'd be here if it was, but this morning I made some enquiries in the village and then walked up to the moor and looked across—and saw you come out and stand at the door.'

The man with binoculars that she'd thought was a bird-watcher—Jancy remembered him now and wondered why she had felt no premonition at the time. You would have thought that when the man you loved more than life itself came near you would have felt some awareness. And she still loved him so much, so much. Her eyes went to his face and then quickly away, afraid that he would see.

Getting up, Duncan came and stood over her, tall and menacing, his physical presence filling the room as Rob's had never done. 'So you see, having spent that much effort to find you, it's hardly likely that I'm going to go away until I get what I want.'

'What do you want?' she asked, gazing up at him in fascinated apprehension.

'I told you: an explanation.'

'And that's all?'

Again he gave that menacing smile. 'For the present.'

Jancy stared up at him, and then, unable to bear him standing over her like that, she slipped under his arm and stood up. 'You can't stay here; there isn't an inn in the village.'

'But I didn't mean in the village—I meant here, in this house.'

'But you can't possibly!' She gazed at him in horror.

'Why not?'

'Because this is my house and I refuse to let you, that's why not.' But he only laughed mockingly. Desperately she said, 'And the people here have very old-fashioned ideas; they wouldn't approve of our being here together.'

Duncan gave a genuine laugh of surprise. 'Do you really expect me to care about that?' Lifting his hand he caught her chin and tilted up her face. 'Especially after all we've been to each other,' he added meaningfully.

Jancy jerked her face away, her hair swirling about her head, catching the rays of the sun. A thought occurred to her and she said triumphantly, 'You can't stay here anyway—Vicki is coming up to visit me for Easter.'

'Good,' Duncan returned shortly. 'Then she can act as chaperon and keep the local gossips quiet.'

'But there isn't room for you.'

'So I'll sleep on the settee, or on the floor. I'm here and I'm staying.'

Realising that arguing wasn't going to get her anywhere and longing to be alone to think, Jancy turned to leave the room, but as she reached the door Duncan called her name.

She stopped but didn't look round. 'Well?'

'Why have you given up your career?'

She swung round to face him, overcome by the question, but before she could answer it, Duncan came up and took hold of her arm. His jaw thrusting forward tensely, he said, 'Did that damn swine who took you from me make you pregnant and then leave you? Did he? Is that why you're wearing these shapeless clothes?' And he yanked up her sweater to look at the outline of her figure.

'No!' Jancy hit out at him in fright in case he saw the truth. 'Don't touch me! Leave me alone.'

Stepping back, Duncan stared at her, his eyes dark pits of hell. 'That's the second time you've said that to me. Do you find me so repulsive, then?' She couldn't answer, could only stare at him, until he said viciously, 'I want an explanation from you—and an apology. I'm going to stay here and I'm going to make you damn well *grovel* to me. Do you understand? *And I don't give a damn what I have to do to get it!*'

CHAPTER FIVE

THE silence that followed Duncan's outburst was one of shock—for them both. Anger, jealousy and bitterness might have festered in his heart for months but this was obviously the first time Duncan had ever put his feelings into words. He drew back, his body trembling, his hands clenched as he fought to regain control.

Jancy couldn't look at him. She knew that if she did she wouldn't be able to resist going to him and giving him the love and reassurance he so desperately wanted. From somewhere she found the strength to turn away and walk out into the kitchen.

He followed her a few minutes later, his emotions again under taut restraint. 'I left my car down the lane. I'll bring it up to the house. And don't get any ideas about locking me out because the way I feel at the moment it would give me great pleasure to break the damn door down.'

Her face very pale, Jancy changed her shoes for boots and put on an anorak.

'Where do you think you're going?'

'Down to Rob's,' she replied as calmly as she could.

'What for?'

She didn't answer, just gave him an expressive look, and Duncan said bitterly, 'You must be very fond of him.'

'He's a friend and a neighbour.'

'Nothing more?'

'No.'

'But he'd like to be.'

Jancy ignored that and pushed open the door to leave the house and stride down the lane.

Catching her up, Duncan said tersely, 'Don't think that you can run away from me again.'

'I know that.' She gave a mirthless laugh. 'I wasn't even going to try.'

He had left his car halfway between the cottage and Rob's farm, where the grass verge widened at the entrance to a field. Jancy gave the car a brief glance and saw that it looked well loaded, as if he'd been prepared for a long search. Maybe it had already been a long search. Her heart bled at the thought, but somehow she pushed it away. She mustn't let him see that she cared—for both their sakes. She had made up her mind on a course of action and had to stick to it. There could be no going back now; the lie was too big, had caused too much hurt. The only way was to go on pretending.

Duncan stopped by his car but watched her as Jancy walked down to Rob's farm. The back door was open as it always was during the day, and she went through the immaculately tidy kitchen to what Rob called the back parlour. He was standing at the window, the one that looked up to her cottage, and didn't turn round when she came in. She stood awkwardly in the doorway for a moment, then said, 'May I use your phone?'

He nodded. 'You know where it is.'

Crossing the hall, Jancy went into the room that Rob used as his office; again everything was orderly and neat, without any clutter of papers on the elderly roll-top desk. She dialled Vicki's number and presently her friend's voice answered, but it was only a recording on an answerphone asking her to leave a message.

The urgency in Jancy's voice plain to hear, she said, 'It's Jancy. Please come up here as soon as you possibly can. Duncan has found me and I need your help. You can leave a message for me at this number if you need to.' And she read out Rob's number.

Slowly she replaced the receiver, wondering if there was anything else she could do, but could think of nothing. Rob was still standing at the window when she went back.

'How's the eye?' But he only shrugged. 'Oughtn't you to put a raw steak or something on it?'

Rob gave a short laugh. 'A waste of good meat.' He turned away from the window to look at her, his face still cold and withdrawn. 'Who is he?'

'He's—he was my fiancé.'

His eyes widened. 'You were going to marry him?'

'Yes.'

'What happened?'

Jancy hesitated for a moment, then said, 'I walked out on him.'

'What did he do to you?'

'Nothing. It wasn't him. I just—I just left him.'

'Something must have happened. He must have done something.'

'No. It wasn't Duncan's fault. It was nothing to do with him.'

'Did you fall out of love with him?'

It would have been easy to say yes, but there had been a slight resurgence of hope in Rob's voice which she didn't want to encourage, so she said firmly, 'No.'

He frowned. 'You mean you're still in love with him?'

Jancy didn't answer. She crossed to stand beside him and look out of the window. Duncan had taken the car up to the cottage and was unloading it.

'You must have had a reason for leaving him,' Rob probed. 'Does he know why you left him?'

Jancy shook her head. 'No. I didn't tell him the true reason.'

Rob looked at her in bewilderment for a moment, then said, 'You were heart-broken when you came here. You looked so thin and——' He stopped abruptly. 'Were you ill? Do you have that illness . . .?' His weather-beaten features blanched and he couldn't finish.

Jancy turned to stare at him, her body tense, her face suddenly very pale as she thought that he had guessed the truth. 'Illness?'

'You know. That terrible illness they have in cities—AIDS.'

Jancy's body relaxed and she was even able to give a small laugh of relief. 'No. No, I don't have AIDS, Rob.'

She turned and walked out of the farm, began to climb back up the hill, thinking that she was a lot luckier than some. She had always known it at the back of her mind of course, but when you were ill yourself it tended to drive the plight of others from your mind. Coming to the field entrance where Duncan had parked his car, Jancy stopped and leaned on the gate, looking across the moor. She had noticed the way that Rob had instinctively recoiled from her when he thought she might have AIDS—would Duncan recoil from her in the same way if she told him the truth? It was an unbearable thought. Glancing across at the cottage she wondered if she could bear to go back there, be so near him. Her fingers tightening on the pitted wood of the gate, Jancy realised that she had only to open it and she could run across the moor, just keep running until she lost herself in the mists, and never come back.

The idea grew in her mind, filled it, until she could see herself running across the heather-clad hills in the sunlight, leaving behind this gross disfiguration of a body that had so betrayed her, leaving behind all the fears for the future, all the pain and grief. Slowly, almost in a trance, Jancy's hand reached out to the iron latch of the gate. Crisp footsteps sounded on the lane behind her and Duncan came up to her. Her hand moved away from the latch, the moment gone as if it had never been.

'Well?' he said shortly. 'How was he?'

'What?' For a moment she couldn't think what he meant. 'Oh. OK. He'll have a black eye.'

'Serves him damn well right!'

'Does it?'

Duncan looked at her for a moment then shook his head. 'No, he was only trying to defend you. But I'm not in the mood for apologising.' Coming to lean on the gate beside her, he, too, looked out across the hills. 'Why didn't you go back to London after he got tired of you and kicked you out, this man you ran away to?'

Jancy sighed, realising that he wasn't going to let up. 'I didn't want to.'

'So you admit he kicked you out,' Duncan pounced.

'I'm admitting nothing. Think what you like.'

She went to turn away but he caught her arm. 'I thought I knew you,' he said forcefully, his eyes holding hers intently. 'I would have staked my life on knowing that you were good and clean and decent. If anyone had told me that you were capable of walking out on me for another man I would have laughed in their face—after I'd taken the hell out of them for smearing your name. I thought that you were loyal and honest. I believed that you loved me.' Despite himself his voice grew unsteady and his fingers bit into her arm, but it was her right arm and didn't hurt.

She gave a small shrug. 'Maybe everything happened too quickly. Maybe we didn't have enough time to really get to know one another.'

'You mean that I didn't have time to find out you were promiscuous,' Duncan said in a return to sneering contempt.

Jancy turned on him at that, flames of anger in her green eyes. She went to speak, but remembered that he had every reason to think it true and her gaze faltered.

'That caught you, didn't it? I suppose you just consider yourself to be liberated. Isn't that what girls call it when they sleep around?'

'I don't sleep around,' Jancy answered unhappily.

'No?' Duncan's eyes narrowed as he looked at her averted profile. 'Then who was he, the man you went away with? Someone from your past? Or someone you met while you were away on that last modelling assignment in Greece?' When she didn't reply he angrily turned her round to face him. 'I've checked with everyone I could find who went on that assignment with you. They all said that you lived an exemplary life out there, going to bed early every night, no drinking, no romance. But they could have been lying; they would have lied if you'd asked them to. Was it one of the crew? Was it?'

'No.' She shook him off, then looked into his haggard face and made one last desperate attempt. 'Duncan, please don't go on with this. Go home and find someone else. Forget me. Forget we ever met. Can't you see that this is destroying you? It's become an obsession.'

'Then I'll just have to play it out until it's no longer an obsession, won't I?' Duncan returned shortly. 'And I'm not leaving until you tell me the whole story, in every detail. That—and anything else I want.'

She gave him a baleful look, wondering if she could make up a story to tell him, but knew that it wouldn't be enough; his anger went so deep that he wouldn't be satisfied until he had subjugated her sexually, too. It was her walking out, her physical rejection of him, that had hurt his masculine pride most of all, and she doubted if he would ever forgive her for it.

But she mustn't let him get near her. Lifting her head, Jancy faced him determinedly and said, 'I have a witness to prove that you've already attacked me once. If you touch me again I'll have you arrested for rape.'

His eyebrows rose and he deliberately let his eyes run over her before he said sardonically, 'You might always consent.'

'I'll *never* consent.' She saw the disbelief in his eyes and added forcefully, 'I mean it, Duncan.'

His mouth became a thin line in his grim face. 'So now we both know where we stand, then.'

It was an ultimatum on both sides. But it was also stalemate. After a long moment Jancy turned and went back to the cottage, Duncan falling into step beside her as they walked silently along. Going in through the back door, Jancy hung up her coat in the little back hall off the kitchen and changed back into shoes, then stood indecisively for a moment, wondering how to cope with the situation. Duncan made up her mind for her by saying, 'I'll take my things upstairs. Which is my room?'

'Find it yourself.' Jancy went to go into the kitchen but a thought occurred to her and she ran upstairs and locked herself in her room. Going across to her bedside table she picked up the photograph of Duncan and herself that she always kept there. Even in hospital it had been beside her bed. It had been taken by Duncan's father, a keen amateur photographer, on the weekend when they went down to his parents, the weekend after they had become engaged. Taken out of doors, the photo showed Duncan with his arm round her and they were looking at each other and laughing, happiness radiant in their faces. It was windy and her hair had blown into a glistening copper halo about her head, but one errant tress lay across her cheek and Duncan was reaching up to brush it away with the back of his hand.

Jancy touched the photograph tenderly, as if a firm touch would hurt the happiness in their faces. She must hide it. She was lucky that Duncan hadn't searched the house and seen it. If he had he would have known that she still loved him. Where could she hide it? Jancy looked worriedly round the room. On top of the wardrobe? Or inside a handbag? No, those were too obvious places.

Duncan banged on the door and she clutched the photo to her in sudden fright. 'Jancy?'

'What do you want?'

'What about the bed and the curtains in the spare room?'

'You want to use the room—you deal with them.'

'Such charming hospitality,' he exclaimed sarcastically, but Jancy heard him go into the spare room at the back of the house and presently the sound of an electric drill as he put up the curtain rail.

Giving a sigh of relief, she pulled the bottom drawer completely out of a chest and put the photo in the space beneath it, then replaced the drawer. She would miss the photo, she thought, then realised how stupid that sounded when the real man was here in the house. But this man wasn't the Duncan she had fallen in love with, this man was the other side of the coin, a man obsessed with anger and the need for revenge. She shivered, afraid of what the days ahead might bring, but comforted herself with the thought that Vicki would soon be here. They were such close friends that Jancy knew Vicki would hear the desperation in her voice and come as soon as she possibly could. And Rob, although he was angry with her now, would always be within screaming distance.

I must be practical, Jancy told herself. I must live from hour to hour, from day to day. And that wouldn't be so difficult: it was what she had been endeavouring to do ever since the operation, ever since she had walked out on Duncan; taking each day as it came and trying to make the best of it.

Endeavouring to be practical, Jancy's first thought was of having to sleep in this room tonight with Duncan only a few feet away, but she resolutely pushed that thought aside. OK, second thoughts: he would be hungry and want a meal; they would have to sit next to one another at the table and eat, unable to avoid looking into each other's eyes. All right, put that thought aside, too. She would cope with those when the time came. What else was there? Oh, no! There was only one bathroom. They would have to share! She imagined herself walking from the bathroom in just her robe and Duncan coming out of his room and seeing her. And he could hardly fail to notice that one breast had gone unaccountably missing.

Dropping down on to the bed, Jancy tried to work out a way that he wouldn't see her. There was a wash-stand in the corner of her room so she was OK to wash and clean her teeth, and if absolutely necessary she supposed she could have an all-over wash and forgo her daily shower or bath. The only other way to do it was to go into the bathroom in the morning fully dressed and come out again the same way. Lord, what a rigmarole. It would be almost funny if every-thing weren't so tense and close to flashpoint.

The construction noises had stopped and she heard Duncan go downstairs and up again a couple of times. Bringing up his things, presumably. It seemed as if he'd brought enough stuff to move in permanently, not just stay for a short while. But then, she didn't know how long he did intend to stay. How long it would take before he would give up on her and go home. She stirred uneasily, wondering whether he had taken a holiday from his father's company and how long he had got. Well, sitting here wouldn't find out. Taking a deep breath, Jancy unlocked the door and went down to the kitchen.

Duncan came down immediately after her, carrying Rob's bag of tools. 'I take it these belong to your friend down the road. What's his name, by the way? We never got round to being introduced.'

'Whose fault was that?' she said tartly. 'His name is Robert Linton, and yes, those are his tools.'

His mouth twisting into a wry grin at her tone, Duncan said, 'Maybe I'll take them down to him.'

'No!' She swung round on him. 'You leave Rob alone. He's nothing to do with this.'

'How quickly you leap to defend him,' Duncan sneered, but added, 'All right, I'll leave them till to-morrow.' He went through into the front hall and pushed open the door to the other front room, looking in. 'What's this room?'

Reluctantly Jancy followed him, standing in the doorway. 'It's what my aunt used as a posh parlour when people came to call.'

'And this?' He looked in the other back room. 'A dining-room by the look of it.'

'Yes.'

'It doesn't look as if you use it very much.'

'I don't.'

'Why not?'

'It's silly eating in there alone; it's easier for me to have my meals in the kitchen or the sitting-room.'

'How about when you entertain?'

She gave a bitter little laugh. 'I don't—entertain.'

His grey eyes came swiftly to her face at her tone and she quickly went back into the kitchen, afraid of having given her loneliness away. But Duncan followed her and said, 'Doesn't anyone come to call?'

'No.' Jancy opened the fridge and took out a pack of eggs.

'Not even your friend down the road, Rob?'

'We occasionally have a snack lunch together if he's working here, but he doesn't come for formal dinners, if that's what you mean.'

Duncan was half sitting on the big, scrubbed pine table that took up most of the centre of the room, his eyes fixed on her face. 'Don't you have *any* visitors?'

'Only unwanted ones, it seems,' she said pointedly.

But he wasn't to be put off. 'What about Vicki? You said she was coming—or was it a lie?' he added derisively.

'No, she is coming. She'll be my first guest. That's why I bought the furniture for the spare room.'

Coming over to the table, Jancy broke eggs into a bowl and began to whisk them up for omelettes. Duncan watched her silently while Jancy tried to concentrate, but her eyes were inexorably drawn to his and her hand stilled. Their thoughts were the same, she realised: that this could have been the oast-house down in Kent, and her preparing a meal, if they had married. A contented scene of domestic happiness instead of this cat-and-mouse game of defiance and retribution.

'What—what happened to the oast-house?' The words were dragged from her.

Duncan's eyes grew as bleak as the snow that lingered on the high moors. 'What the hell do you care?' But then his hands clenched and he said, 'I still have it. There was no point in restoring it and I haven't got round to reselling it.'

Each word, spoken in such cold tones was a cutting rebuke. Jancy flinched away from them and busied herself with preparing the meal, but her hands shook as she worked. She was unable to get used to the fact that Duncan was *here*, that he had finally found her.

She set places at the end of the kitchen table where she usually ate, and cut slices from a home-made loaf of fresh granary bread to eat with thick soup from the pot that simmered on the Aga. 'It's ready,' she said shortly, as she set the steaming soup bowls on the table.

It seemed weird to sit down beside him at the table, to eat, knowing that whenever she looked up Duncan would be there, solid, real, instead of the dream figure that she had so often longed for. Jancy's hand shook convulsively and she had to put down her spoon.

Duncan glanced at her and his voice grew scathing as he said, 'What's the matter—lost your appetite?' Adding with mock concern, 'I'm not putting you off your food, am I?'

Her hands balled into tight fists beneath the table, Jancy strove to control herself and presently picked up her spoon and began to eat again. But he was right; he had driven away her appetite.

'You said that Rob Linton works here: what did you mean?' Duncan demanded.

'He helped me to get the house fit to live in again and now he's working on the garden,' Jancy replied, glad of something else to think about.

'You pay him wages?'

'No.'

She shook her head and went to go on but Duncan said in sharp, self-inflicted pain, 'What do you do, then—work it off?'

Anger brought her chin up and she said curtly, 'If you'd let me finish I would have told you that Rob is into veteran cars. My aunt left me an old car and

Rob and I agreed that he would work here to pay for it rather than giving me cash. It suits us both that way.'

'I see. I beg your pardon.' But Duncan didn't sound at all apologetic. 'And how much longer does he have to work before he pays for it?'

'I don't know. Rob will tell me when the time comes.'

Duncan's mouth twisted in wry amusement as he reached out for a piece of bread. 'It sounds a very loose arrangement. But perhaps Rob likes it that way; it gives him *carte blanche* to come up here and lust after you whenever he wants.'

He was goading her, Jancy knew. Trying to push her into losing her temper in the hope that she would tell him what he wanted to know. But the fact that he was searching for a confession that just wasn't there helped Jancy to control her feelings a little. It disturbed her, though, that Duncan should have immediately realised the position between her and Rob. OK, Duncan was exaggerating it, but he was basically right; she had known that Rob was falling for her and had been too wrapped up in her own sorrows to do anything about it. She had let it drift when she should have made it plain that there was no future in it. Well, Rob knew now, anyway, she thought resignedly.

'Did you make this bread yourself?'

'What?' Jancy surfaced from deep in her own thoughts. 'Oh. Yes.'

'Such self-sufficiency,' Duncan remarked sarcastically. 'I'd never have believed you had it in you.'

She gave him a straight look. 'Wouldn't you?'

His eyebrows flickered but he held her gaze. 'What happened to the ambitious model who was heading for the top? The career girl who hardly ever had food in the house because she always ate out? What happened to the shining hair and the beautifully made-up face? What happened to the bright, fashionable clothes?'

Jancy put her left elbow on the table and held her arm in front of her. 'Have you finished your soup?'

She reached to pick up his bowl but Duncan caught her wrist. 'I asked you a question,' he said fiercely.

'I know. I . . .' She turned her head away, trying to hide the sadness that came into her eyes. She must look terribly different, she supposed, with her face devoid of make-up, and her hair pulled back and tied with an old piece of ribbon. He must think her quite ugly. For a moment it hurt unbearably, but then Jancy realised that it would help the situation if he found her abhorrent. So she shrugged and said, 'What's the point in dressing up in a place like this? The sheep on the moors don't care what I look like, and quite often they're the only living creatures I see from one day to the next.'

'So why stay here?' Again the probing question.

'Because it's what I want. I'm happy here,' she lied bravely.

'Rubbish! The only reason you came here was because you were too darn scared to go back to London and face me. That's the truth, isn't it?'

Shaking off his hand, Jancy stood up. Picking up the soup bowls she put them by the sink and brought over the omelettes and bowl of salad that she'd made. 'You think too darn much of yourself,' she retorted as she sat down. 'My coming here had nothing whatever to do with you.'

'So why did you come?'

She gave him a tired look. 'It doesn't matter how much you probe, Duncan, I'm not going to tell you anything I don't want you to know. So why don't you just eat your dinner and shut up?'

His mouth drew into a grim line. 'You think you've got the upper hand, don't you? But I'll wear you down until I *make* you tell me the truth,' he threatened.

His eyes met hers challengingly and it was Jancy who looked away first. She put an unsteady hand up to her forehead and rubbed it as if she had a bad headache. They ate the rest of the meal in a taut silence, although Jancy actually ate very little, just pushing her food round the plate and being careful not to look at Duncan again. But she couldn't help but be aware of his growing tension and wondered uneasily if it was just because they were together or whether there was some special reason.

When the meal was over Jancy cleared the table and began to do the washing-up. Duncan helped himself to a coffee from the pot and stood watching her, making no offer to help. She could sense the electric anticipation in him as he watched her so morosely and she deliberately took a long time, hoping that his mood would change.

But strangely he seemed to find amusement in her dragging out of the simple task. In the end there were no more dishes left to wash and wipe, no more surfaces to clean, and nothing left to put away. Reluctantly Jancy wiped her hands and hung the towel on the bar in front of the Aga to dry. She glanced at Duncan's face and felt a *frisson* of fear; there was a black devil in his eyes; he had planned something and could afford to wait, had all the time in the world until he sprung his trap.

Suddenly she was angry, tired of being the mouse and deciding to be the cat for a change, and maybe she could learn something in the process. Leaning back against the sink, Jancy crossed her arms over her chest and said in a casual, almost conversational tone, 'Have you been in Yorkshire long, looking for me?'

'A couple of weeks.'

'Really? Where did you go first?'

'That hardly matters,' Duncan responded, his voice sharpening.

'No, I suppose not. Must have been frustrating for you, though.'

'Not when it achieved its purpose.'

'But you haven't—and you won't,' she said tauntingly.

His eyes narrowing, Duncan said, 'My main purpose was to find you.'

'Oh, yes, of course. And just how long are you planning on staying here?'

'As long as it takes.'

'What about your work? You can't stay away from that indefinitely.'

'That needn't concern you,' he said crisply.

'I bet it concerns your father. How long has he given you?'

Duncan glowered at her. 'I told you; that's nothing to do with you.' He straightened up. 'Do we have to stand here in the kitchen?'

But Jancy was gazing at him wide-eyed. 'You just walked away from it, didn't you? I bet as soon as you got that short list of addresses you just told your father to hell with the job, and came up here.' His jaw tightened, confirming her guess. 'I was right,' Jancy said hollowly. 'You *are* obsessed.'

'And don't I have the right to be?' Duncan demanded with sudden fierceness. 'Do you know what it was like being in New Zealand and not being able to contact you? And then having my mother call and say that you hadn't kept your date with her, that you'd left a letter for me at my flat and your ring in a box beside it?' Putting out his hands Duncan caught hold of her shoulders and shook her, his eyes mirroring the remembered pain. 'Well, do you?'

Jancy shook her head helplessly. 'No. I——'

'No, of course you don't. And you can't imagine what it was like to move heaven and earth to get the job done as soon as I could and fly home, dreading to read your letter but always hoping at the back of my mind that it was some terrible mistake.' He paused, striving to control the raggedness in his voice. 'And then I read it. Just those few cold lines to end what had been the most wonderful thing that had ever happened to me. What I'd waited all my life for. Just a casual, "I'm sorry, but I've found someone else."' His fingers tightened and Jancy gasped, but nothing would stop him now. 'And that's when the real hell started. When I pictured you with some other man, doing all the things to you that I thought we had done in a love that would last forever. Holding you. Touching you.' His eyes, dark and tormented, came up to glare into hers. 'But, no, you deceitful little bitch, how could you possibly imagine what I've been going through? And don't tell me ever again that I have no right to be obsessed!'

He shook her again in burning anger and Jancy cried out, '*Stop it!* You're hurting me.'

For a moment he looked pleased, as if he enjoyed hurting her, but then he pushed her away from him in disdainful contempt.

Jancy fell back against the wall, rubbing her left shoulder, her face white, taking deep breaths against the pain. Duncan, still full of his own bitterness, turned his back on her and it was several minutes before either of them recovered. When Jancy spoke the sick look had gone from her face, but her mind was full of his confession—for it had been a kind of confession, that agonised outburst of pain and bitterness. He wouldn't have told anyone else, would hardly have let them see it. Perhaps only the close members of his family would have realised how deeply he had been hurt.

Slowly Jancy said, 'So you *did* walk out of your job.'

'Of course,' Duncan returned harshly, swinging round to face her. 'Not that I was of much use there lately anyway. I'd had too much time off while I was trying to find you, and when I was there I couldn't concentrate properly.'

Feeling compelled to say something, all Jancy could find was an inadequate, 'I'm sorr——'

But Duncan cut her off. 'Don't say that!' he exclaimed forcefully. 'You don't mean it—and it certainly isn't enough.'

'But you said you wanted an apology from me,' Jancy reminded him, her eyes on his face, her voice low and uncertain.

'I said I was going to make you grovel—and I'm far from doing that yet. When I've finished with you,

you'll go down on your knees and *beg* me to leave you alone.'

'And do you really think that's going to make any difference? I could do it now but you wouldn't go,' she said with a return of spirit. 'You know full well that you intend to stay here until you make my life an utter misery. You went through hell, so I have to go through it too. And your asking about the man I went to is just a masochistic wish to turn the knife in your wound so that you feel justified in hurting me. You just want your pound of flesh. You——' She broke off suddenly, remembering the pound of flesh that she had already lost. 'Oh, God!' She put her head in her hands and pressed her fingers into her skull.

Duncan came over to her and pulled down her hands, staring at her anguished features. 'Yes, maybe you're right at that. Maybe that's what I came here for.' He put a hand under her chin to tilt her head back. 'And maybe I'm already starting to get what I want.'

It took a supreme effort of will not to burst into tears. But maybe it would have been better if she had; it was what he wanted. Instead Jancy said in a sad, heavy voice, 'I don't know you any more.'

Letting her go, Duncan stepped back from her, his face drawn. 'You think I've changed?'

She shook her head and said on a long sigh, 'I don't know. Maybe you haven't. Maybe there was a side of you that I never saw either.'

'In other words, we're well rid of each other.'

A look of pain came into her eyes, but Jancy pushed herself upright and somehow managed to face him defiantly. 'Yes, we certainly are. The sooner you realise that and go home, the better for both of us.'

Softening her voice, she said persuasively, 'I know what I did was wrong, Duncan, but I *had* to do it, and I really thought it would be easier for you if I made a clean break. OK, I realised that you'd be hurt and angry, but surely that was better than dragging things out and you trying to make me change my mind.' She looked at him pleadingly but he was watching her, his eyes narrowed, and didn't speak. 'Usually if people are angry they get over a broken affair more quickly. Anger is surely better than—better than heartache and despair,' she said brokenly.

His voice harsh, Duncan said, 'And that's all you think it was, do you—a broken affair? Well, it was far more than that to me.' His face twisting with bitterness, he went on, 'You were the love of my life. I'd never wanted any woman as I wanted you. Never wanted to make any other woman my wife. I would gladly have given my life for you. But you tossed it all back in my face with just a few words of explanation and went off with your—your what? Your new lover? Or was he just someone you fancied going to bed with?'

'I don't have to listen to this,' Jancy said shortly and went to walk out of the kitchen, but he barred her way.

'Oh, this is nothing,' Duncan said sadistically. 'I haven't even started yet.'

Unable to take any more, Jancy went into the hall and stood for a moment with her hand on the newel post, trying to find the strength to go upstairs. But Duncan came up behind her and put a hand on her arm. 'You look tired. Come and sit down for a while.'

She gave him a perplexed look, taken aback by the sudden gentleness in his tone. His face was carefully

bland but he couldn't completely hide the flare of
anticipation in his eyes. Doubtfully, she held back,
but Duncan was already leading her towards the
sitting-room.

'Do you have a television?'

Puzzled and suspicious, Jancy allowed him to draw
her into the room as he opened the door and switched
on the light. 'No, I——'

She broke off, staring. Then gave a great cry of
pain, her hands going up to her face. *'Oh, no!'* In
the centre of the room, where it caught the most light,
Duncan had placed his easel, and on it was the
unfinished portrait that he had painted of her, the
one in which she represented a stone sculpture. In
which her breasts were white as alabaster, firm and
youthful, the nipples delicious little rosebuds of
colour. Whole and beautiful.

Another great cry of anguish was torn from her
and Jancy whirled on Duncan. 'My God, you're
cruel!'

Astounded by her reaction, Duncan nevertheless
said curtly, 'If I am it's because I was taught by a
past master—or should I say mistress?'

Her body shaking convulsively, Jancy burst out,
'You think *you've* been hurt, but you've hardly
touched the surface! I know *exactly* what it's like to
lose someone you love. You want to punish me, but
there's nothing, *nothing* you can do that will hurt me
more than I've been hurt already!'

CHAPTER SIX

JANCY ran out of the room and up to her bedroom, stumbling from side to side as she went up the stairs. She managed to turn the key in the lock but then her strength suddenly gave out and she slumped to the floor, leaning her back against the door. Crossing her hands over her chest, she gripped her arms, digging her fingers into her flesh, trying to hurt herself physically to take away the pain in her heart. Seeing the portrait, remembering how she had posed for it in pride of her own body and in deep love for Duncan, had made all the terrible torture of loss come back, multiplied a hundredfold. Then she had been elegant and serene, full of life and vitality, now she was just an empty, broken shell. She began to cry, her body swaying in despair, her head resting on her knees, but in such deep distress that her throat was too rigid to let the racking sobs burst through.

'Jancy?' Duncan's voice sounded immediately behind her, startling her as he rapped on the door.

'Go—go away.'

'I want to talk to you.'

'*Go away!* Leave me alone.'

He tried the handle but found it locked. Unnerved by his being so near, Jancy crawled away from the door on hands and knees and dragged herself up on to the bed, burying her face in the pillow so that he wouldn't hear her cry. Duncan banged on the door a couple more times but she didn't answer and he even-

tually went away. Jancy cried until she was exhausted
and then fell into a sleep that was full of tormented
dreams.

When she woke the room was in the deep darkness
of night. Automatically Jancy reached out to turn on
the bedside light and saw that it was nearly three in
the morning. She felt terrible. Her eyes ached and her
throat felt sore from crying. And the room was cold.
Shivering, she went across to the window that she had
intended to open just for a short time to air the room
and had completely forgotten. After shutting it, Jancy
went to close the curtains but, glancing down the
hillside, she saw that there was also a light on in one
of the upstairs rooms of Rob's farm. His bedroom,
she supposed, never having been upstairs in his house.
It was the middle of the lambing season; perhaps he
had been out attending to a sheep. Or perhaps he
couldn't sleep and was, like her, looking out of his
window up to the cottage, wondering what was happening between her and Duncan.

Resolutely she pulled the curtains, shutting out Rob;
she had enough to handle, she couldn't cope with Rob
as well. Taking off her outer clothes, Jancy went over
to the hand basin and washed her face and bathed
her eyes, letting the cool water run down her arms.
Slowly she towelled herself dry, then reached up
behind her and unhooked her bra, catching the prosthesis with a practised movement of her left hand as
she did so. Wearing it all day made her ache and she
was glad to take it off. She held it in her hand, looking
down at the falsie, still hating it but unable to ignore
it. Made of silicone, it looked like a piece of breast-
shaped jelly, even having the slight suggestion of a
nipple, and was quite heavy. To the touch, it was as

soft and pliable as her flesh had been, and was very similar in colour. The manufacturers had done their best to make a substitute that was as near the real thing as possible, but this was an instance when a substitute could only enhance a loss, not replace it.

After putting the prosthesis away in the box where it was kept when not in use, Jancy went to take her nightdress from under her pillow, averting her eyes from the mirror over the dressing-table as she passed it as she always did. But tonight she stopped, hesitated for several minutes, then switched on the main central light, and went over to the Victorian full-length mirror that had belonged to her aunt. This she had pushed into a corner when she first arrived so that she couldn't possibly see herself in it, but now Jancy pulled it into the centre of the room and stood in front of it. Slowly she reached out to tilt it so that her whole body was reflected in its rich, silver depths.

It was the first time she had ever attempted to look at herself and it was a few minutes before she could bring herself to do so. She took a glance and looked quickly away, feeling sick. Gritting her teeth, Jancy forced herself to look again. Pretend it isn't me, she thought. Pretend it's a photograph. Of a stranger. A complete stranger. Go on, look. It can't hurt you to look. Slowly, reluctantly, she turned her head and opened her eyes, her emotions fighting her mind. It isn't real. It isn't you. So you can admire the neat scar. How many stitches did they take out? Thirty-five. Right from the centre of the chest and up under the arm. It's fading now, not burning red any more. The surgeon did a very good job on this person who's in this mirrored picture. Even if he couldn't save her figure he saved her life. Hopefully.

Her eyes had been concentrating on the scar to the exclusion of all else, but then Jancy's eyes moved fractionally to the right as she looked at her whole breast, still as firm and tip-tilted as before. Suddenly she let out a strangled cry and swung the mirror down. It would have been better to have *both* breasts amputated than to have one good one forever reminding you of what might have been. Better to be completely flat-chested than to go around wearing that disgusting falsie for the rest of your life!

Grabbing up her nightdress, Jancy pulled it on. One of her aunt's, it was high-necked and long-sleeved, made of flannelette and a complete passion-killer. But it was warm in the cold, northern winters—and she had a much surer way of killing any passion she might arouse.

She slept again, eventually, but felt so heavy-headed when she woke at nine-thirty that it was an effort to keep her eyes open. Left to herself, Jancy would probably have stayed in bed, but Duncan was here and a sense of guilt, as well as a longing to see him again no matter what, made her get up and dress, putting on a long, loose skirt and the usual layers of sweaters, before going downstairs.

He wasn't in the house. There were signs that he had eaten breakfast, and she ran upstairs and saw that his things were still in the spare room, but he definitely wasn't anywhere around. He wasn't in the garden or the yard either; Jancy looked out of his bedroom window to see. His car was still there, though, so he couldn't have gone far.

Turning away, she saw that the bed had been neatly made. The pillow was cold when she pulled down the covers and touched it, so he must have been up for some time. Her hand trailed over the pillow, trying to capture his essence. There were no pyjamas to touch; he never wore night clothes, although he had liked to see her in a glamorous nightie on the few occasions that they had spent a whole night together. Not that it had ever stayed on very long. Her face lit for a moment, remembering, her eyes great green pools of wistful yearning. Sighing, she carefully replaced the covers and smoothed them down.

Duncan's things were laid out neatly on top of the mahogany chest of drawers: hairbrush and comb, battery razor, aftershave. Jancy sniffed the latter, the fresh, masculine tang evoking a hundred memories. Her fingers tightened but she was devoid of tears. Replacing the cap, she heard a door shut downstairs and went out on to the landing. Duncan was in the front hall with a foot on the first stair, his hand on the newel post.

'Found what you were looking for?' he asked sardonically, when he saw her come out of his room.

His tone helped. Her chin rising, Jancy said, 'Unfortunately, yes. I hoped you might have left.' Going down the stairs, she saw that he had a basket of shopping at his feet, so he must have been to the shop in the village.

As she came down into the better light, Duncan looked at her closely. She had made no attempt to hide the haggardness of her face, knowing that no make-up could disguise the deep dark shadows round her eyes and the hollowness of her cheeks. His eyes widened as he looked at her, but then his eyes drew into a frown. 'You look as if you didn't sleep,' he said roughly.

'Well, that should please you.' She walked past him into the kitchen. 'I see you've been shopping.'

'Yes.' He put the basket on the kitchen table. 'You haven't got enough in that fridge to keep a bird alive.'

'I wasn't expecting you to arrive,' Jancy pointed out tartly. 'If you'd let me know you were coming I'd have got Rob to kill a cow and a few sheep.'

Duncan gave her a grim look. 'A sleepless night doesn't seem to have affected your temper any.'

'Was it supposed to?' Jancy filled the coffee percolator and switched it on.

Ignoring that, Duncan said, 'Why did you get so upset when you saw the portrait?'

Having expected that to be his first question, Jancy was able to smile grimly and say, 'Did you think it was the picture that annoyed me? No, it was just the fact that you seem to be taking over the place.'

He didn't believe her; she hadn't really expected him to, but it was the best she could do. Jancy busied herself putting away the shopping he'd brought. There was quite a lot of it, so he obviously expected to stay for quite some time. He'd even bought wholemeal flour, too.

Seeing her looking at it in surprise, Duncan said, 'It was on your shopping-list,' and he gestured towards the wipe-clean board on the wall.

'Oh. Of course. How domesticated of you.'

His lips thinned and she wondered why she was riling him like this. Because he expected it, she supposed. Because she was living a lie and the part she was playing called for her to defy him and make him go away. And it was so much easier, by defying him and keeping him at a distance, to hide her true feelings.

After pouring her coffee, Jancy sat down at the kitchen table.

'Please don't bother to pour one for me; I'll get it myself,' Duncan said sarcastically.

She merely gave him a look and he sat down at the table beside her, his coffee in a mug with a picture of an owl on it. Duncan studied her strained profile for a moment, then said, 'I thought you might have had a newspaper delivered, or collect one from the shop every day, but the woman there said you never buy one. And you have no television either. You're becoming quite a recluse.'

'I have a radio,' Jancy said on a defensive note.

'Really? Where?'

She tried to remember when she'd last listened to it, but couldn't. 'It's around somewhere.'

'Have you no interest in what's going on in the world?'

Jancy looked down at her coffee, both hands round the mug, thinking about it. World news somehow didn't seem important when your own world lay in broken pieces around your feet. The weather forecast was of no moment when you could look out of your window and see for yourself. Even local news didn't matter when you never went anywhere. Events happened, laws were passed, politicians argued, fashions changed; but here in this remote part of Yorkshire it all seemed totally irrelevant. Maybe he's right, she thought, maybe I am becoming a recluse. 'No,' she answered at length. 'I don't think I have.'

'You've changed,' Duncan commented, giving her a frowning look. 'What made you change?'

'Life, I suppose.' Getting up, Jancy went over to a cupboard and took out a bottle of aspirins, taking out two and swallowing them down with her coffee.

Duncan watched her silently, then said, 'That's a very ambiguous remark. Perhaps you'd care to be more explicit.'

There had been a threatening note to his voice that made Jancy smile wryly. 'No, thanks.'

Immediately his hand came out and gripped hers. 'What happened when you ran away from London?'

Startled, her dark-smudged eyes came up to meet his grey ones, finding them fixed intently on her face, a look of grim determination in their ice-cold depths. She sighed, knowing that he wouldn't be satisfied until she made up some story. 'All right, if you really want to know.' She paused, trying to think of something that would convince him. 'You were right: someone I used to know, someone I was in love with, came back into my life while you were away. I realised that I was still crazy about him so I moved in with him. It was as simple as that.'

Duncan's features were drawn very tight and his eyes were still fastened on her face. 'You brought him here?'

She hesitated a second, but knew the lie would be too easy to disprove. 'No, I went to his place. In Paris,' she chose at random.

'He's French?'

'Yes.' And so could stay safely as a figment of her imagination, she thought thankfully.

'What happened?'

She shrugged. 'The same as the first time; it just didn't work out.'

'Why not?'

Jancy gave him an irritated look; her imagination wasn't up to this, especially this morning. 'Why don't things work out? We weren't emotionally compatible. We wanted things from each other we couldn't give.'

'But physically you were compatible?' he said sardonically.

Hastily she looked away. 'That side of it was OK, I guess.'

'Well, you should know!'

She gave him a fiery look, angered by his heavy sarcasm. 'Yes, it was fantastic, if you must know.'

'He must have been quite a man.'

'Yes, he was.'

'What was his name?'

'What?' Jancy was completely thrown.

'I said what was his name? You ought to know that.'

'Of course I know it,' she snapped. 'But I don't intend to tell *you*.'

He switched to another tack. 'Did you leave him— or did he kick you out?'

Her green eyes gave him another smouldering look. 'I left him!'

'How long were you with him—finding out whether you were compatible this time?' Duncan demanded sneeringly.

'About three months.' Jancy picked the period out of thin air, thinking that it gave some credence to the story.

'So why didn't you go back to London?'

'I'd let my flat; I had nowhere to live.'

'So you left him and came here?' He fired the questions relentlessly.

'Yes.'

'But why come here? It's hardly your scene.'

She tried to divert him, saying belligerently, 'How would you know what my scene is?'

But he didn't take the bait. 'All right, so you came here to lick your wounds. But why cut yourself off like this? And why let yourself become so thin and dowdy?'

Jancy drained her coffee-mug and went to stand up but Duncan put a restraining hand on her arm.

'You haven't answered me.'

She gave an exaggerated sigh. 'I was getting over a broken love-affair. I didn't want other people. I wanted to be alone to—to try and regain my confidence, to decide what I wanted to do with my life. I needed time to think.'

'And is that what you did before?'

'Before?' she said uncertainly.

'You said that this man—this Frenchman—was an old lover. That you'd had an affair with him before and it had broken up.'

'Oh. Yes.' Jancy tried desperately to think. 'Well, the first time I—I knew he wasn't serious, but this time I thought—I hoped it would be for keeps. And when it didn't work out I was naturally very upset.'

'Oh, naturally,' Duncan agreed with infinite sarcasm. 'But of course you'd done the right thing and left him.'

'Yes.'

'Liar!' He suddenly leaned forward, startling her. 'Why don't you tell the truth?'

'Th-the truth?' Jancy instinctively backed away from him.

'Yes. Admit that he used you and then kicked you out when he tired of you.'

'No, I . . .' She started to protest, but then thought, Oh, let him believe whatever he wants to believe, and she hung her head as if he was right.

'So now we're getting to the truth. That's why you came here and shut yourself away—because your pride can't take the fact that he doesn't want you,' Duncan said triumphantly.

Slowly Jancy lifted her head and looked at him. 'Can yours?' she said steadily.

Duncan's face whitened. *'Touché,'* he said shortly. Getting up, he went to stand by the window, looking unseeingly out.

Jancy watched him, noting the hard thrust of his jaw, the way his knuckles showed white as he gripped the window-sill. Her heart was wrung and she looked sadly away, hating to have to lie to him and just hoping that now he would be satisfied and go home.

At length he turned and came to stand beside the table. 'So it looks as if we're both in the same boat.'

She nodded. 'Yes.'

He sat down again, looking at her almost with new eyes. 'You seem to have taken it very badly.'

'So did you.'

His mouth twisted. 'Maybe it was the way that you did it.'

'There's no easy—or kind way.'

'No, I suppose not.' Duncan sat and looked at her intently, as if he was trying to read her mind. Jancy bore it for a few moments, then lowered her head, afraid that he might guess that she was lying. 'When are you going back to London?' he asked.

She gave a great inward sigh of relief; he had believed her. 'When I feel up to it,' she answered with a shrug.

'You'll become introverted if you stay up here alone for much longer,' he commented.

'Introverted?' If that meant not telling anyone the truth, then she was introverted already, Jancy thought wretchedly. Making a great effort, she said, 'No, of course I'm not. I just wanted some space to get over a love-affair, that's all.'

'*A* love-affair?' Duncan's voice became harsh again. 'Doesn't what we had count as a love-affair, then?'

Realising her mistake, Jancy said quickly, 'That was different.'

'How—different?'

'It just was, that's all.'

His voice raw with self-inflicted pain, Duncan said scathingly, 'I see. You mean it was just a gentle, unexciting relationship, do you? It wasn't the kind of earth-shattering experience that lifted you to the heights of passion, the kind that you would remember for as long as you lived.' He got to his feet, pushing the chair over as he did so. 'I'm sorry. You should have told me. Strangely enough, I thought you enjoyed it at the time. Which just shows you how wrong you can be— or was it just that you were good at pretending?'

Jancy couldn't let him think that; no matter how many lies she had to tell, she'd never tell that one even if it would drive him away. He had turned away, unable to bear to look at her. Getting quickly to her feet, Jancy went to him and put her hand on his arm. At her touch a convulsive tremor ran through him, but he didn't turn round. 'That isn't true and you know it,' she said forcefully. 'You're experienced: how could I possibly have pretended without you realising? No woman could possibly fake what I felt— what you made me feel.' She paused, her eyes dark with pain and spoke truthfully, from her heart. 'What we had was very, very special. It was beautiful. Perfect.'

He had turned to stare at her. 'Why then——?'

With a sigh Jancy switched back to lies. 'It was too perfect to last. Can't you see that? It was wonderful, like a dream come true. But you can't live in a dream. When you went to New Zealand I faced up to reality and saw that being a housewife in the country just wasn't for me. I was too young to settle down. I—I didn't want to be tied, to that kind of life or to—or to one man. When—when Pierre came on the scene I went with him to escape from married domesticity as much as anything.'

'And now you're reduced to this,' Duncan pointed out harshly with a sweeping gesture. 'What happened? Did running away to him rebound on you? Did you fall head over heels in love?'

'Something like that,' she admitted tartly.

'Then you couldn't possibly have been in love with me. Not really in love, or you'd never have looked at another man.'

'Maybe it was the dream I was in love with,' Jancy admitted hollowly.

'Maybe you were at that.' Duncan stared at her for a moment then strode over and gripped her arms. 'But I wasn't in love with a dream. I loved you and wanted you—for the rest of my life.' He gazed down at her, his eyes dark and tormented, his voice ragged. And it was inevitable that he should pull her to him and kiss her with a savage cruelty that brooked no denial.

Jancy tried desperately to resist, to stand rigidly in his hold as his mouth raped hers, forcing her lips apart. But, no matter how hard she tried to fight it, the flame of desire that she had so ached for in these long, lonely months leapt into instant life, sending great tremors of awareness coursing through her love-starved body. She felt as if she had come alive again, been reborn. A low moan broke from her and she made a last feeble attempt to push him away, but Duncan put his hand in her hair, pulling it free from its confining ribbon, and holding her prisoner beneath the insistent conquest of his mouth.

It was impossible for him not to recognise the re-action he had aroused in her, impossible for him not to pursue it. His body trembled. He had waited so long for this moment, had lived it a thousand times in his mind. Putting a hand low on her waist, Duncan held her close against him, his kiss becoming compulsively demanding. Jancy's mind whirled, taking her away from the present into the past, when he had held her like this and the future had stretched endlessly before her, full of love and happiness in the safety of his arms. She gave a low animal moan and moved her hips against his, the deep-down ache of yearning craving for fulfilment. Duncan gasped, and his lips left hers to rain kisses on her face, his breath hot and panting. Taking his hand from her hair, he covered her breast.

For a moment Jancy didn't realise, could feel nothing, but then she gave a great cry and pushed him violently away. Drawing back in terrified dread, she covered her chest protectively with her folded arms. 'Don't! Keep away from me. Don't ever touch me again!'

She screamed the words at him, then whirled and ran out into the yard, somehow pulled open the gate, and went running down the lane towards Rob's farm, her hair flying about her head in the breeze.

Had he guessed? Did he know? Jancy leaned against Rob's fence-post, panting for breath, her eyes going back up the lane in fear to see if Duncan was coming after her. He had come out of the cottage and was standing by the gate, watching, but making no attempt to follow. With a gasp of relief, Jancy ran across to the door and let herself into Rob's kitchen.

'Rob! Rob, are you there?'

'In the office.' Quickly he opened the door. 'Are you all right? Has he hurt you?'

'No.' Somehow she managed to pull herself together. 'No, I'm all right. My—my friend; has she phoned yet?'

He shook his head, his eyes going over her flushed, haggard features. 'Not yet. I would have brought the message up—you know that.'

'Yes, I . . .' She tried to smile. 'It's just that I'm so eager to hear from her. Sorry to bother you; I can see you're busy.'

'Not too busy for you. Did you come out without a coat? You'd better come near the fire. It's about time I had a break,' he said, without looking at his watch. 'Want to join me in a coffee?'

She nodded gratefully and sat on the old armchair near the fire in the kitchen, her body still trembling. Going to the sink, Rob held the kettle under the tap. 'Have you sorted things out with your boyfriend yet?'

'No.' He had turned to ask the question and she saw him fully in the light. 'Oh, Rob, your eye!'

'A real shiner, isn't it? He packs quite a punch—your fiancé.'

'*Ex*-fiancé,' she reminded him.

'Well, whatever he is, it looks as if he's going to join us for coffee,' Rob remarked grimly, looking out of the window.

Tucking her feet under her on the chair, Jancy tried to lose herself in its depths as Duncan knocked briefly on the door and came in. His eyes flicked over her in anger, not pity or rejection, and Jancy knew with profound relief that he hadn't guessed the truth. He turned to Rob. 'You left your tool-box behind yesterday. Thought you might need it so I brought it down.' The box was heavy but he carried it easily over to a corner and put it on the floor.

'Thanks. Want a coffee?' Rob said grudgingly.

'Please. Black and no sugar.' Duncan's eyes settled on Jancy. 'You seem to be quite at home here.'

'Jancy's welcome here any time she wants to come, she knows that,' Rob said before she could speak. 'She's been coming to this farm ever since she was a little lass and used to stay with her aunt for holidays.'

Duncan's brows drew into a frown. 'You've known her that long?' He looked round the kitchen, seeking a woman's touch and not finding it. 'You live here alone?'

'Since my wife and boy died,' Rob returned curtly.

They both looked at him, Jancy wondering whether, even after all this time, it still hurt for him to say that. She knew that having to tell people that she was no longer engaged to Duncan would hurt unbearably for the rest of her life.

'I'm sorry about the eye,' Duncan said, his voice much milder.

Rob nodded. 'You seem to have come off best.'

He made the coffee and gave Jancy a cup, then put the other two mugs on the table. He sat down and, after a moment's hesitation, Duncan sat beside him.

'Come far, have you?' Rob asked him.

'London.'

'And what do you do in London?'

'I'm an architect.'

Jancy had expected Duncan to resent Rob's questioning, but he showed no sign of it. She sat quietly in the chair, only half listening, while the two men talked, feeling each other out. She had come to know Rob well during the last few months. He wasn't good at hiding his emotions, he was too open for that, and she could recognise his feelings from his tone of voice. When Duncan mentioned that his hobby was painting, she heard a note of respect come into Rob's voice, the sort of respect that a man who worked with his hands had for a man who worked with his brain or who was creative. Rob's own self-respect for the way he lived and the way he did his job was high, Jancy knew, and he took pride in running the farm. But he knew he would never be able to create something beautiful, could never design a building or paint a picture, and he had an awed respect for those who could. For a moment she felt a little jealous, but then was glad; at least it meant that they wouldn't fight again.

Hearing her own name mentioned, she glanced up and found Duncan looking at her.

'I've painted one portrait of Jancy,' he was saying. 'And I was getting on quite well with another, but she—er—left before I'd finished it. As a matter of fact I've brought it with me. You'll have to come up and see it.'

Jancy threw him a withering look, but before Rob had a chance to reply the phone rang in his office.

He muttered a word of apology and went out to answer it. Jancy kept her eyes fastened on her coffee-cup, but could feel Duncan's gaze and had to fight not to look up.

'You'll have to face me some time,' he said scathingly.

'The call's for you, Jancy,' Rob said, coming back into the kitchen. 'Your friend from London.'

Jumping to her feet, Jancy ran into the office and closed the door behind her. 'Vicki?'

'Yes. What's happening up there? Who answered the phone?'

'My neighbour. How soon can you come? I really need you. Duncan's here and I can't manage him alone.'

'Why don't you come here, then?'

'I can't. He won't let me. He—he's out for revenge, Vicki.'

'As bad as that, huh?'

'Worse.'

Vicki came to a snap decision. 'OK. I have a date tonight but I'll ditch him and come up straight away.'

'Oh, Vicki, you're an angel!'

'I'll come up by train, so you'll have to meet me at the station.'

They discussed times and Jancy arranged to pick her up at York that evening. 'Vicki, I can't thank you enough,' Jancy said fervently.

Her friend laughed. 'I just can't wait to find out what all this is about. See you later.'

Jancy replaced the receiver in infinite relief, but she still had to get through the rest of the day. As she walked back into the kitchen, the eyes of both men rose to look at her.

'That was Vicki,' she said into their expectant silence. 'She's coming up today.'

'Answered your SOS, did she?' Duncan said sardonically.

Ignoring him, Jancy turned to Rob. 'Thanks for the coffee.'

He nodded and stood up. 'Maybe I'll come and take a look at that portrait.'

As they all three walked back up the lane together, Jancy didn't know whether to be pleased that Rob had come with them or not. She was glad of his protection, feeling that she needed it now more than ever, but she wasn't at all sure that she wanted him to see the portrait. The picture not only showed her partly naked but it gave too much away; every brush-stroke was a caress, executed with love and tenderness; and the love that she felt for Duncan shone from her eyes, plain to see.

When they reached the cottage Duncan opened the door of the sitting-room for Rob to go in first and was about to follow when Jancy said, 'You'll have to move out of the guest room.'

His eyebrows rose. 'I'm surprised you don't tell me to clear out again.'

'Would you go?'

'No.'

'Then what's the point?'

Going upstairs, Jancy busied herself by changing the sheets on the spare bed, trying not to think of the two men downstairs, looking over the portrait, each seeing her with different eyes. When she'd finished she went into her bedroom where she brushed her hair,

put on a little make-up, and collected a long camel
coat and a hat.

The men were still in the sitting-room when she
came down. Jancy glanced at Rob, met his reluctant
gaze, and flushed a little; in his eyes decent women
just wouldn't pose for a picture like that.

'Going somewhere?' Duncan asked.

'Yes, to York. I have shopping to do and then I'm
going to meet Vicki from the train.'

'I'll get my coat, then.'

'You don't have to come; I can manage alone,'
Jancy said without much hope.

Duncan laughed and said grimly, 'If you think I'm
going to let you out of my sight, you're crazy. I only
have your word for it that Vicki is coming today, and
I wouldn't put it past you to get on a train and take
off again.'

Jancy bit her lip and raised wide, vulnerable eyes
to meet his. 'I have nowhere else to run to,' she said
simply.

He gazed at her for a moment, his eyes puzzled,
frowning, but then his face hardened. 'One could
almost feel sorry for you,' he said mockingly. 'Except
that I'm beginning to know you too well, and I'm not
going to fall for your petty feminine tricks.'

He went to get his overcoat and Rob gave Jancy a
direct look. 'Will you be all right with him?'

'Yes, I think so. Vicki will soon be here.'

He helped her on with her coat, then held her arm
for a moment. 'Will you tell me why you ran away
from him?'

She hesitated, aware of Duncan moving around upstairs. 'I don't want to—but I will if you insist on
knowing.'

'Have you told Duncan yet?'

'No.' She shook her head. 'Not the truth. I haven't told anyone the truth.'

He had been looking into her shadowed green eyes and saw the deep sadness there. 'You don't have to tell me,' he said roughly. 'Not if you don't want.'

Duncan came downstairs and she locked up the house and said goodbye to Rob.

'We'll go in my car,' Duncan said peremptorily.

She didn't argue; she didn't feel much like driving anyway after the sleepless night. Duncan's car, a Jaguar XJS, was far more comfortable than hers. Taking off her hat, Jancy leaned back against the head-rest, grateful for the efficient heater. The powerful engine ate up the miles to the ancient county town and, despite the tension of being with Duncan, Jancy began to doze. But it was a troubled sleep, she stirred several times and murmured disjointedly, then woke with a start to find Duncan's hand on her shoulder, shaking her.

'What? What is it?' She started away from him.

'We're here.' He gave her a strange look. 'You sounded as if you were having a nightmare.'

'Oh. Did I—did I say anything?' she asked, trying to sound casual.

'Not much that I could understand. You seemed to be afraid of something. You kept saying no, and . . .'

'What else?' She looked at him in fearful anticipation.

His grey eyes met hers in a puzzled frown. 'You kept saying my name.'

Jancy could find nothing to say to that. She looked quickly away and gathered up her belongings.

York was more noted for its beautiful Minster, its museums and quaint old streets than for its shopping facilities, but Jancy managed to buy the luxury bath foam and other beauty products that she knew Vicki used, and which she hadn't bothered to buy for herself. She also bought a new mirror for the guest room and a bedside lamp. Duncan came along with her, his mouth set into grim lines, and Jancy knew exactly what he was thinking: that they would have gone together on shopping trips like this to furnish the oast-house if she hadn't run out on him. She dragged the shopping out until the stores closed at five-thirty but then there was still over an hour to wait before Vicki's train arrived.

'We may as well get something to eat,' Duncan suggested.

They found a place that did afternoon teas but said very little during the meal. The other customers talked and chatted, laughed and clattered their teacups, but their table was a circle of taut, uneasy quiet. Jancy kept her head lowered, deliberately avoiding his eyes, but she could feel his sub-surface anger. Suddenly, out of the blue, he said sharply, 'You're not immune to me, Jancy; this morning proved that. And Vicki's being here will make no difference—I'll still get what I want, no matter how long it takes.'

She shook her head. 'Vicki will stay as long as I need her.'

'Until I give up, you mean?'

'Yes.'

Leaning forward, Duncan said intently, 'I'll never do that. You can try and hide behind Rob or Vicki, but I'll still be here, waiting. Always waiting, Jancy. Remember that.'

At seven Duncan drove to the station and Jancy got out and strode on to the platform without waiting for him. The train came in a few minutes later, on time, and Vicki got out of the first-class coach, a man opening the door for her and helping her out. She looked great, her hair a mass of casual curls, her clothes smart and expensive.

'Vicki!' Jancy ran to meet her and gave her a big hug, tears of relief in her eyes. 'Oh, I'm *so* glad you're here.'

'So am I; it was quite a journey.' Vicki turned to thank the man who was now unloading her luggage; there seemed to be an awful lot of it. 'Thank you so much, that's awfully sweet of you. If you could just carry it outside for me...'

'There's no need; I'll take it.' Duncan came up to them. 'Hello, Vicki.'

'Duncan! How lovely to see you again. Jancy did mention that you were here.'

Duncan's lips twitched in wry amusement. 'I imagined she had.'

He picked up the cases and Vicki gave Jancy a look of astonished enquiry behind his back, but Jancy shook her head. 'I'll tell you later,' she mouthed.

But there was no opportunity for the two girls to be alone until after they had arrived back at the cottage and Jancy took Vicki up to her room.

Shutting the door, Vicki said, 'Good, it's warm in here. I was afraid it would be dreadfully spartan so I brought loads of sweaters and woollen tights with me.' She sat on the bed and drew Jancy down beside her. Her eyes went over her friend. 'You're really having a bad time of it, aren't you? How long has Duncan been here?'

'Only since yesterday,' Jancy answered, thinking that it seemed like a lifetime.

'Well, if he can do this to you in a day, then it's a good job I came.' She put a comforting hand over Jancy's. 'Now, tell me everything.'

'It's as I told you—Duncan found me and he's out for revenge. It would have been impossible to keep him at arm's length without you here.'

'I see, he wants *that* kind of revenge, does he? Well, I can't say that I blame him, Jancy; he was crazy about you. I've never seen anyone so distraught as when he came to my place looking for you.'

'I know. It's my fault. But I thought I'd hidden myself away so that he would never find me.'

Vicki stared at her in puzzlement. 'Even going so far as to give up your career? Just why did you walk out on him?'

'That hardly matters now. I've given him an explanation but he isn't satisfied with it.'

'What explanation?'

Jancy sighed. 'I made up a story that I hoped would be enough to make him leave, but he won't go.'

'Why make up a story, why not tell him the truth?' Vicki pursued. 'Come to that, why not tell *me* the truth?'

There was nothing Jancy would have liked better, but she knew that Vicki would understand her anguish only too well and be deeply distressed, and she didn't think that her friend would be able to hide that distress from Duncan. 'If Duncan leaves, I'll tell you then,' she promised. 'But not now—just in case he makes you tell him. At the moment he thinks that I ran away to live with an old flame, a Frenchman.'

'And am I supposed to know this Frenchman?'

'It might help if you said that you'd met him,' Jancy
acknowledged.

'So what's his name?'

Jancy stared at her. 'Oh, lord, I've forgotten what
I called him. Paul, I think.'

Vicki laughed. 'Well, you'd better be right. OK, I'll
back you up all I can, and I'll make sure to keep the
wolf from your door tonight. Do you think Duncan
will leave now that I'm here?'

'I was hoping he would, but he said that he was
going to stay for as long as it takes,' Jancy said
dispiritedly.

'Then we'll just have to make things so tough for
him that he'll be glad to go,' Vicki said determinedly.
'Don't worry, I won't leave you alone with him, so
he'll have no opportunity to start a fight—or anything else.'

'Thanks,' Jancy said huskily. 'You don't know what
a relief it is to have you here.'

'My pleasure. Now, I'd better unpack.' She stood
up but saw that Jancy was looking at her with an
intent, pleading expression in her green eyes. 'What
is it?' And she sat down again.

'There's something else I want you to do for me.
It's a lot to ask, I know, but if you would . . .'

'So what is it?'

Taking hold of her hand, Jancy gripped it hard as
she said compellingly, 'I want you to guard me against
Duncan, but there's something else as well—I want
you to seduce him.'

CHAPTER SEVEN

'WHAT?' Vicki goggled at her. 'You want me to sed——'

'Hush, he'll hear you.' Jancy quickly put her hand over Vicki's mouth. 'Yes. Don't you see? It's the only way we're going to get him away from here and keep him away.'

'But that's crazy. It's you he's in love with; he isn't going to even look at another woman while you're around.'

'Yes, he will,' Jancy said steadily. 'Precisely because I'm around. He'll do it to make me jealous. He wants to hurt me and he'll jump at the chance.'

Vicki shook her head. 'I think you're wrong. I think he has more integrity than that.'

'Ordinarily, yes. But these aren't ordinary circumstances, Vicki. He's had months to let the hurt fester and nothing will satisfy him but to hurt me in return.'

'This is a crazy set-up.' Vicki gazed at Jancy for a long moment. 'What the hell went wrong? I thought you two were really in love. You seemed to have everything going for you. It's not as if Duncan was forcing you to give up your career, even. And then you just suddenly take off and shut yourself away in this——' she waved her hand expressively '—this god-forsaken place. What did he do to you?'

'Nothing. It had nothing to do with Duncan.' She leaned forward urgently. 'Honestly, Vicki, I didn't leave because of Duncan.'

'He isn't kinky, or anything?'

'No, of course not. He's dead straight. For heaven's sake, Vicki, you've only got to look at him to know that. Will you do it? Will you get him off my back?'

But Vicki hesitated. 'I'll think about it. Give me some time. Not that I think it's even possible with you around.'

Jancy smiled tiredly. 'Nonsense. You can seduce any man you want, you know that.'

'Be careful,' Vicki warned laughingly. 'I'm a sucker for flattery. And now you'd better help me unpack; if we don't go down soon Duncan will start thinking *we're* kinky.'

They unpacked Vicki's cases with the speed of experience, Jancy trying very hard not to feel jealous when she saw some of the gorgeous clothes that Vicki had seemed to think necessary for a holiday in the wilds of Yorkshire. When they came downstairs they followed the savoury smell of cooking that met them and found Duncan in the kitchen, standing over the Aga.

He glanced round and said sardonically, 'So you've finished your heart-to-heart at last? I was beginning to think I'd have to eat all this food myself.'

'Mm, supper.' Vicki walked over to him. 'I'm starving. It smells great. What is it?'

'Beef Stroganoff. Sit down and I'll dish up.'

'Anything I can do?' Vicki offered, but Duncan had already set the table and opened a bottle of red wine.

He put a heaped plate in front of Jancy, but she looked up and said, 'I can't possibly eat all that.'

Ignoring her, Duncan said to Vicki, 'She's much too thin, don't you think? She hardly eats anything.'

Annoyed, Jancy retorted, 'I've lost my appetite since you turned up.'

Vicki glanced from one to the other of them. 'Look, if you two want to needle each other, fine—but would you mind not doing it at mealtimes? It gives me indigestion.'

Duncan gave a wry grin. 'Sorry. I wouldn't want to spoil your appetite, too.'

'This is very good,' Vicki commented. 'Do you always cook for yourself?'

She succeeded in diverting him and kept a conversation going throughout the meal. Jancy deliberately didn't join in so that the comparison between Vicki's vivacity and her own taciturnity would be even more marked. But Duncan glanced at her several times, his voice dying, his eyes abstracted, until Vicki regained his attention.

It was late when they'd finished eating. Jancy went to put a plug on the lamp she'd bought in York for Vicki's room, but Duncan took it from her.

'Here, let me do that.'

'I can put on a plug—I'm not helpless.'

He merely gave her a chauvinistic look and did the job neatly and efficiently in half the time it would have taken her. 'Anything else you want done?'

'I didn't want that done.' Then, reluctantly, 'Thanks. No.'

He nodded. 'Then I'll collect my things from guest room and make up a bed on the settee in t. sitting-room.'

Jancy went to bed expecting to have another sleepless night, but perhaps it was the fact that Vicki was there, or just that she was completely exhausted, but she soon fell into a deep, and for once dreamless, sleep.

Because there were no other houses nearby, Jancy often left the curtains open at night, and so she was wakened the next morning by a shaft of sunlight that lay across the bed. Opening her eyes, she listened lazily to the sound of sheep calling to their lambs, of birds singing lustily as they made their nests under the eaves. It's spring, she thought, and felt a resurgence of optimism and vitality course through her veins. But then she remembered that there would be no spring for this ugly husk she had become, and had to fight off an overwhelming feeling of bitterness and despair. Quickly, without giving herself time to mope, Jancy got up and, in case there was anyone around, dressed, went into the bathroom where she got undressed again to have a bath, then put her clothes on a second time to go downstairs and make breakfast.

She was the first person down and took her mug of coffee out into the garden where she sat on a seat that caught the morning sun. Not long afterwards Duncan came to stand in the kitchen doorway. He watched her for a few moments, then stuck his hands in his pockets and ambled over. 'Mind if I join you?'

For answer, Jancy merely moved further along the bench seat, making space for him. There was plenty of room on the seat but he deliberately sat down right xt to her so that his shoulder rubbed hers. He was earing jeans and a loose sweater over his shirt, and she caught the tangy aroma of his aftershave. She felt his strength, his power, the sheer vital masculinity of him. Desire suddenly raged through her, filling every pore of her body, overpowering in its intensity, the most potent sexual yearning she had ever known. Her hands gripped the mug so hard that her knuckles were transparent and she closed her eyes tightly for a moment, as if she found the morning sunlight too strong.

When she opened them Duncan was watching her, and Jancy had the unbearable feeling that he had guessed what was happening to her. She stood up quickly. 'What would you like for breakfast?'

But he reached out and caught her hand. 'Don't go yet. You were enjoying the sun.' His voice was unusually gentle—unusual for the last couple of days, at least.

It would have been so easy, so unbelievably, exquisitely wonderful, to do as he asked. To sit close beside him as if they were still lovers. Taking her hand from the warmth and comfort of his, Jancy shook her head.

With a frown of anger, Duncan rose to loom over her menacingly. 'What did he do to you, this man?' he demanded. 'And don't try and tell me it was nothing. You wouldn't be in this state if it was just a broken affair.' His voice was rough, but Jancy recognised that it wasn't entirely anger, there was a note of concern for her there, too.

'You're mistaken. I'm OK.' She turned to go in an saw Vicki looking out of her bedroom window. Jancy waved and Vicki opened the window.

'Hi, you two. What a lovely morning. See you downstairs in ten minutes.'

Jancy went in to make breakfast and made sure that she wasn't alone with Duncan again for the rest of the day. In fact, she contrived as much as possible to leave Vicki and Duncan together, a ruse that he saw through immediately and did his best to frustrate. Vicki tried to help, but it was difficult when the three of them were in such a small house. In the evening Jancy rather desperately suggested going down to the pub in the village for a drink. 'We can pick up Rob on the way. He's my neighbour,' she explained to Vicki. 'I'm sure you'll like him.'

'Don't say that!' Vicki exclaimed. 'It's always guaranteed to make you hate the person on sight.' Then she laughed. 'But I'm willing to give him a try on your recommendation.'

Rob came with them willingly enough, but was rather overwhelmed by Vicki. When they reached the pub the two men went to the bar to buy drinks, leaving the girls sitting at a table near the big inglenook fireplace.

'How did Rob get that black eye?' Vicki asked at once. 'It looks comparatively new.'

'It is,' Jancy answered ruefully. 'He and Duncan came to blows the day Duncan arrived.'

'How come?'

Jancy sighed. 'How do you think? Rob thought Duncan was attacking me so he pulled him off and they started fighting.'

'Good heavens! Rob doesn't look the type to get into a fight.'

'He's a Yorkshireman, deceptively quiet until roused.'

'Is he, now?' Vicki said with a laugh. 'I'll have to remember that.'

It was impossible to be sad when Vicki was around. Jancy grinned at her. 'Hey, it's Duncan you're supposed to be flirting with, not Rob.'

'I haven't agreed to that yet.' Vicki glanced across at the bar. 'And somehow I don't think I stand much chance with either of them—they're both obviously potty over you.'

Surprisingly, the evening turned out to be an enjoyable one. Vicki set out to amuse both men and Rob was soon at ease, laughing at her deliberately outrageous stories. Duncan, too, often laughed, but his eyes were constantly going to Jancy as she sat quietly in her seat, very willing to let Vicki sparkle and be the centre of attention. Ordinarily Jancy would have been as full of vitality as her friend, and, to someone who had known her as she used to be, the change was very marked. Especially to Duncan who had known her better than anyone, and who had made her so happy that she had radiated a love of life.

It was Saturday night and there were quite a few locals in the pub. After a couple of hours and several pints of strong Yorkshire ale, one man got to his feet and gave them a monologue in a broad accent that they could only just understand. It was a bit risqué and made everyone roar with laughter. Then someone else jumped up and sang a rousing rendition of 'On Ilkley Moor' with everyone joining in the chorus so

loudly that Jancy was sure they could have been he~
in the next valley.

The impromptu entertainment went on until we~
past closing time, so it was gone midnight when they
finally left. It was a clear night, the moon almost full,
and the promise of spring that had come with the
morning still mellowed the air.

'I want to cross the stream by the stepping-stones,'
Vicki announced.

'We call it a beck,' Rob told her, adding, 'You'll
break your leg if you slip in those high heels.'

The 'high heels' were only an inch or so and to Vicki
and Jancy were hardly heels at all.

Vicki laughed. 'One of you men will have to stand
guard, then.' And she looked at Duncan.

'If you think I'm going to wade through the stream
just in case you fall, you're crazy,' he replied promptly.

'Such gallantry!' Vicki sighed theatrically.

'I'll go ahead of you,' Rob offered, and was re-
warded with a dazzling smile.

Jancy stood on the bank beside Duncan, watching
their progress, putting her hands to her mouth in
horror when Vicki nearly slipped, then laughing and
clapping as Rob grabbed her. When they were safely
across she turned to walk up to the bridge but Duncan
was in the way.

'That's the first time I've seen you so much as smile
since I've been here,' he said shortly.

She glanced up at him, about to make a sharp
retort, but saw the bleakness in his eyes. With a sad
shrug, she said, 'The—circumstances don't make for
laughter.'

'I thought you'd forgotten how.'

The remark surprised her because it was almost true; laughter hadn't been a part of her life for a long time now. I'm turning into a miserable old frump, she thought in sudden anguish. Stepping round him, she strode quickly over the bridge and caught up with Rob, leaving Vicki to wait for Duncan.

'Will you come for lunch tomorrow?' she invited.

Rob smiled, pleased, but said, 'I have to go out over the moors and check on the flocks tomorrow.'

'All right, we'll make it dinner, then.' An idea occurred to her. 'And perhaps we could come out on the moors with you and help.'

'All of you?'

'If the others want to come. May we?'

'Aye—but tell yon lass to wear a pair of sensible shoes.'

They had reached his gate and he waited to say goodnight to Duncan and Vicki as they came up, then the three of them walked on to the cottage. Jancy made a bedtime drink, leaving the others in the sitting-room. She took as long as she could over it, giving them time alone, but Duncan came into the kitchen to find out what was happening.

'I'm tired,' she told him abruptly. 'I'm going to drink mine in bed. Perhaps you'd take Vicki's drink in to her?'

She knew she hadn't fooled him, but Duncan said, 'OK,' and took the tray.

When Vicki came upstairs a few minutes later she knocked on Jancy's door. Jancy was already undressed but quickly pulled on a loose housecoat, bunching it up to hide the flat half of her chest. When she opened the door Vicki pulled a face. 'Duncan's dispatched me up to bed with my drink. Can I come in and chat?'

'Sure. Here, you take the chair.' Kicking off her slippers, Jancy got into bed and pulled the blankets up to her chin.

They talked about the evening and Rob, both of them tacitly avoiding the main issue, until Vicki finished her drink and yawned. 'I'm bushed. Is there anything planned for tomorrow?'

'We're going on the moors with Rob to look for lambs.'

'Really?' Vicki looked pleased. 'I think I might enjoy that.'

They all did, driving over the rough tracks across the moor in Rob's old Land Rover, then getting out to walk as they searched among the sheep for any ewes with Rob's mark that had a lamb running at her heels. They found quite a few that Rob daubed with coloured dye to mark them as his, but they had to cover a large area before he was satisfied that he had found them all. As they walked over the moors Jancy stayed beside Rob as much as she could, giving Vicki a chance to work on Duncan. And Duncan didn't seem to mind, making no attempt to change the situation, and often lagging behind, he and Vicki deep in conversation. At lunchtime they ate a simple picnic that Rob had brought of freshly made bread, cheese and beer. They sat in a sunny corner of a field where the angle of the dry stone walls sheltered them from any coolness in the breeze.

The men began to talk cricket and Vicki said to Jancy, 'Let's go and pick some heather.'

'OK, but it's a bit early,' Jancy began, then read the message in Vicki's eyes and got quickly to her feet. 'What is it?' she asked as soon as they had walked out of earshot.

Vicki gave her a warning look. 'I was talking to Duncan this morning. Or rather, he was pumping me, trying to find out how much I knew about your imaginary boyfriend. I said what you told me, of course, and he seemed quite convinced. But that name you gave me was wrong; he pounced on it immediately. I had to say that I'd made a mistake.' She stopped and stooped to pick a sprig of pale purple heather that was showing among the green. Twiddling it in her fingers, she said, 'Jancy, there's something I've been wondering—just how *did* Duncan find you?'

'He said he hired a detective agency to go through everyone in the whole of North Yorkshire named Bruce until he came to a short list of possibles,' Jancy answered flatly. 'Then he came up here to go through those for himself.'

'Good grief!' Vicki gave her an amazed look. 'But it only goes to prove what I'm rapidly beginning to suspect: that on the surface he may seem all out for revenge—maybe he even believes that himself—but I think that deep down he wants you back.' She stopped and looked at Jancy. 'He's still in love with you, Jancy. And no matter what you've done I believe he'll forgive you—that he *wants* to forgive you and start again.'

'That wasn't the impression I got,' Jancy said, remembering his overwhelming fury.

'Perhaps not. You can hardly blame the man for being mad at the way you walked out on him. And

maybe he *needs* to punish you in some way to—
assuage his own hurt.' She shrugged helplessly. 'I don'
know, I'm no psychiatrist, but I do know that Duncan
isn't the type of man to be deliberately cruel. At the
moment he's torn apart by anger at what you did to
him and the fact that he's still in love with you and
can't bear to let you go. Why don't you talk to him,
tell him the truth? Whatever it is, I'm sure if you were
open with him he'd try to understand.'

Jancy smiled and touched Vicki's hand gratefully.
'You're a good advocate, Vicki, but I can't do that.'
She began to walk on and after a few exasperated mo-
ments Vicki caught her up.

'Look,' Vicki persisted persuasively. 'We're pretty
close friends, aren't we? And I know you well enough
to know that you wouldn't have got engaged to
Duncan if you hadn't been head over heels in love
with him. And you certainly wouldn't have agreed to
marry him if there had been another man that you
cared about. I think that you're still in love with
Duncan.' She paused, waiting for Jancy to speak, but
her friend walked on with a bleak, averted face. 'In
fact, I'm *sure* you're in love with him. So why the big
mystery?' Catching hold of Jancy's arm, she pulled
her to a stop. 'Just why did you walk out on him the
way you did?'

After hesitating for a long moment, Jancy said,
'Something happened to me and I can't tell him.'

'Try, give him a chance.'

'I can't.' Shaking her head in distress, Jancy said,
'Please don't ask me to again.'

'I have to. I hate to see you so sad and unhappy
like this. Duncan, too. Why can't you tell him?'

Jancy sighed and looked out across the moors. 'If he weren't an artist I might. But he *worships* beauty and—and purity.'

Vicki stared at her. 'Worships? Isn't that a strong word?'

'No. Once we were talking about where to spend our honeymoon, and Duncan said, "Let's go to Florence. Let's go and worship at the shrine of beauty." And I made some flip remark about beauty being only superficial and not worth his adoration, and he said, "Beauty is the only thing worth worshipping because that alone can truly fulfil the purpose of life. It's greater even than love, although love is beautiful, because there will always be beauty for the eye even though love becomes only a memory." So you see, that's why I can't tell him.' She bit her lip, trying to find the courage to say the words. 'I am—I have been—defiled.'

Vicki gazed at her in wide-eyed horror. 'Are you—are you saying that you've been raped?'

Slowly Jancy turned to look at her. 'Not in the way you mean, no, but I'm not the same person Duncan fell in love with. Believe me, Vicki, if he knew he wouldn't want me any more. It's kinder to lie to him this way than to tell him the truth, it really is.'

Vicki shook her head in perplexity. 'I just don't understand. Won't you tell *me* what happened to you?'

'No, because you'd feel sorry for me and you wouldn't be able to hide it from Duncan. When he's gone, then I'll tell you, as I said.' Her face shadowed. 'I need to tell someone.'

They walked slowly back to join the men an.
they came near, Duncan got to his feet, searching tr
faces. Both girls avoided his eyes and began to pac
up the picnic things, bringing a grim look to his face.

The four of them spent the rest of the day together,
Rob coming to dinner and afterwards taking little
coaxing to give Jancy a piano lesson on her aunt's
old instrument that stood against the wall. They sat
together on the piano stool and Jancy tried to concentrate but was too aware of Duncan and Vicki on
the sofa, talking in low voices, the conversation often
interrupted by Vicki's light laugh. She's flirting with
him, Jancy thought, recognising a particular tone in
her friend's voice. A flare of jealousy ran through her
and she hit a wrong note. 'Sorry.'

'It's all right, you're getting it,' Rob encouraged.
'Try again.'

Jancy looked rather helplessly at the sheet of music
on the stand. 'What did you say that little twiddle
means?'

Somehow she got through the evening, and the next
morning got up early and went for a long tramp over
the moors, leaving the two of them alone whether
Duncan liked it or not. When she got back Jancy
heard the sound of chopping and went round to the
back of the house. Duncan had his sleeves rolled up
and had demolished half her pile of logs, chopping
them into manageable-sized pieces, a job that Rob
had always done for her before.

At first Duncan didn't notice her, he was too intent
in swinging the axe down with a kind of concentrated
fury, satisfying the need to work out his anger physically. When he saw her he paused for a moment,

axe poised at the height of its swing, then brought down so hard that the log flew in half and the axe head stuck in the block. Then he strode over to her, caught her by the arms, and pulled her roughly against him as he kissed her with fierce hunger.

With no time to build any resistance, Jancy was pliant under his mouth. She tasted salt on his lips, smelt the musky scent of manly sweat on his skin. All the basic, primitive instincts of weak woman for the stronger man rose in her and she was filled with an overwhelming need to surrender, to give him what he wanted, here on the grass in the sunlight. For a moment her hands went to his shoulders, her nails digging into him, but then the greater dread of discovery tore her from his hold.

She didn't have to tell him not to touch her again, her eyes said it all as they stood panting, staring at each other. Slowly Duncan lifted a hand and wiped the back of it across his mouth, as if wiping away the taste of her lips. The gesture hurt unbearably. She went to turn away, but Duncan said, 'Where have you been? Vicki was worried about you.'

'For a walk. I like to walk on the moor.'

His voice rough, Duncan said, 'Don't try and fool me, Jancy. I know that you're trying to push me and Vicki together.'

Her head came up. 'I asked her to get you off my back, yes,' she said with unintended cruelty. 'I felt that we needed to—to try and ease the situation. I hoped that by talking to Vicki about—normal things, you would be able to see things in a different light. Realise that what happened was no big deal.'

'It obviously wasn't for you,' he said harshly.

'No.' She looked away.

Duncan thrust his hands in his pockets, mak[ ] great effort to control himself. 'There's still a lot [ ] haven't explained.'

'Does it matter?'

'Yes, it matters!' he retorted on a violent note. 'I'm not going to spend the rest of my life wondering why. Why you walked out on me——'

'I told you.'

'You told me there was another man. This Frenchman. What was his name?'

'His name doesn't matter,' she said in panic.

Duncan's eyes flashed to hers but he let it go. 'But you still haven't told me why you've changed your whole lifestyle. Why you've cut yourself off from everyone like this.' He looked at her intently. 'Are you ashamed, is that what it is?'

'Ashamed?'

'Of having made a fool of yourself over this man.'

Realising that she would have to steer him away from that, Jancy lifted her chin and said, 'No, I'm not ashamed of loving him—and I don't consider that I made a fool of myself. A few months with him were worth giving up everything for. I'm just—devastated that he didn't want me for keeps, that's all.'

Duncan's face had hardened. 'So I don't come into it at all?'

'You already knew that,' she lied, her heart bleeding.

'So I did.' His voice was as cold as glacier ice.

Hoping that it would make him leave at last, Jancy said, 'Your being here is just—a nuisance.'

flinched back at the murderous look that came
his face at that. Hardly able to control his voice,
ancan said, 'Well, I'm afraid that I'm going to go
on being a *nuisance* until I'm good and ready to leave!'
Then he turned on his heel and strode into the house,
his body taut with suppressed fury.

Duncan could hardly bring himself to speak to
Jancy for the rest of that day, so he naturally turned
to Vicki who, after a startled look at Jancy, took full
advantage of the situation. Duncan realised, of course,
but began to deliberately encourage Vicki and to flirt
back himself. That he was doing it to try and hurt
Jancy they all knew, and he succeeded far more than
he could ever hope, could ever guess. To see him put
a familiar arm round Vicki's waist, to hear him
laughing with her, and watch him paying all the little
attentions that she had counted as her own, filled
Jancy with tormenting pain. She tried to avoid them
by going into a different room, but then her imagination ran riot and it was almost worse than reality.

It went on over the next day, too, but that next
evening Vicki suggested that Duncan finish Jancy's
portrait.

'I doubt if she'd sit for me,' Duncan remarked, his
fingers toying with one of Vicki's luxuriant blonde
curls.

'Of course she will. Won't you, Jancy?'

Thinking that it would at least keep Duncan's hands
off Vicki, Jancy reluctantly agreed, but then wished
she hadn't because it meant that Duncan's gaze was
perpetually on her as he began to paint. He didn't
have a lot to do, just her hair and the background, a
few finishing touches. He worked silently, applying

colour, scraping off the excess with a palette k
Jancy's thoughts went back to the happy times, w.
she had sat for him in his studio, and she knew th
Duncan's did, too. She tried to put them out of her
mind, but couldn't, so let them fill her soul.

Standing back from the picture, Duncan looked at
it critically. 'It's done. There's no more I can do to
it.'

'It's great.' Vicki had been quietly watching, but
she got up and came to his side. 'Come and look,
Jancy.'

Slowly Jancy obeyed her. There was something different about the picture, something apart from the
finishing touches. For a few seconds she couldn't see
it, then gave a small gasp as she realised that Duncan
had repainted her eyes. Where they had been full of
love and joy now they were dark pools of sadness.
Her face was still beautiful but the light of life had
gone, leaving her a dejected shell. Bitterly she realised
that for Duncan her beauty had also gone; she was
no longer the woman he worshipped.

It was late when he'd finished. Jancy and Vicki went
up to bed but Jancy couldn't sleep, her heart very
heavy. The hall clock struck one and she heard the
unfamiliar creak of Vicki's door opening. She
expected to hear the other girl go to the bathroom,
but instead Vicki's steps went quietly down the stairs.
Then Jancy heard the door of the sitting-room, where
Duncan was sleeping, gently open and close.

It was what she'd wanted, Jancy told herself. What
she'd connived at. She ought to be pleased. But she
lay in desolate sadness for the rest of the night,

...pless, listening for Vicki's footsteps when she ...ally came back upstairs a couple of hours later.

Jancy didn't ask any questions the next day. Vicki slept very late, which was hardly surprising, and Duncan didn't emerge from the sitting-room until gone ten. Busying herself first with making bread, Jancy then walked down to the village to shop and called in at Rob's on the way back to invite him to spend the evening. Her face taut with tension, Jancy somehow managed to get through the day. Trying not to show how much she cared, how much it hurt. And carefully avoiding looking at Vicki and Duncan so that she wouldn't see the awareness of each other in their eyes.

When Rob came round it was easier. He talked of normal, everyday things, and made Duncan and Vicki laugh with his fund of village anecdotes. They sat round the table, chatting, drinking another bottle of wine, and Jancy began to think that she was going to get safely through the day.

Everything went wrong very suddenly. Jancy was so wrapped up in her own misery that she didn't even see it coming. Duncan idly said, 'Jancy tells me you're interested in vintage cars.'

Rob nodded. 'She let me have her aunt's old car at the beginning of October and I've been working on it ever since.'

None of them noticed the sudden tightening of Duncan's body as he said, 'October?'

'Yes, when Jancy came here,' Rob answered innocently. 'I'd been looking after the car and I asked Jancy the day after she arrived if I could buy it——'

'Did she come here alone?'

'Why, yes, she's always been alone. She
came to a stop, aware of the sudden shattering
that filled the room. He found three pairs of eyes
on him—Vicki's wide and startled, Jancy's fu.
dread, and Duncan's darkening with rage. 'What's t.
matter? What have I said to——?'

But Duncan had swung round to face Jancy.
Grabbing her arm, he pulled her to her feet. 'So there
was no man! No Frenchman whose name you can't
remember. It was all a lie. You came straight here from
London. It was me you ran away from. *Me!*'

'Duncan, please.' Vicki jumped up and tried to
intervene but he pushed her roughly aside.

Looking down into Jancy's terrified eyes, he shook
her roughly. 'You're going to tell me the truth, do you
hear me? I want to know *why*. What had I done to
you to make you run away from me? What was so
terrible that you had to write that damnable note, tell
such cruel lies?' He shook her again. 'Well? Why was
it? You sadistic little bitch, what did I do that drove
you to do this to me?' He shouted the words at her,
his voice raw with anguish.

'Let her go!' Vicki tried to pull his arm away while
Rob stood in the background, struck dumb by the
violent emotions he had inadvertently let loose.

But Duncan didn't even hear her. Pulling Jancy
roughly forward, he yelled, 'You're going to tell me!
You're going to tell me all of it. Did I love you too
much, is that it? Did just loving you make you hate
me?'

'No!' Suddenly Jancy came to life. Sweeping up
her arms she broke free of his hold and stood back,
unable to hold out any longer. 'It was nothing to do

u. It was me. Me!' Tears flooded down her
. 'Oh, why didn't you stay away? Why couldn't
just hate me?' He took a step towards her but
backed away, her body shaking with emotion. 'All
ight! You want to know the truth—I'll show you the
truth!'

Before anyone could stop her Jancy ran into the
sitting-room where the portrait stood on the easel,
Duncan's palette and paints still on the table beside
it. Her trembling, feverish hands scrabbled among the
paints until she found the palette knife, its thin silver
blade long and sharp.

'Jancy, no!'

Vicki's terrified voice came behind her but Jancy
swung round to the picture and hacked with the knife,
stabbing and slicing it until the left breast was completely cut out and lay in pieces on the floor, the nipple
still taunting her with its rosy beauty.

CHAPTER EIGHT

IT WAS Vicki who realised the truth first. She said, 'Oh, no! Oh, no.' And sank down into a chair, her face full of horror.

But Duncan saw only the mutilated picture. 'What the hell did you do that for? What's the matter with you? Why——?'

'Do you still not understand? Do I have to spell it out to you? All right. Then look. Look!' Still crying, Jancy began to pull up her sweater, tearing at her shirt in her hurry. 'Oh, it's all right, Rob, you don't have to turn away. There's nothing to see. *Nothing!*' And on the last word, with a great sob, she pushed aside the prosthesis to reveal the still livid scar across her chest, the flesh completely gone from underneath it.

Rob was frozen into silence, but Duncan said, 'Dear God!' in a stricken voice and started back in revulsion, his eyes fixed on her chest, but then his clenched fist came up to cover his face.

Jancy's head went back, her teeth clamped together, her throat two rigid columns of stress as she fought for control. Then suddenly she pulled her clothes down and ran at Duncan, hitting out at him. 'Get out of here! Go on, get out! Get out!'

Numb with shock, he didn't try to resist but let her propel him out of the room and then through the front door, stumbling down the steps. Then Jancy whirled and ran back to Vicki, who was still sitting in the chair,

, sobbing. 'Get him away from here. Take him
to London. Help him, Vicki, help him.'

'Oh, you poor thing. Oh, Jancy, I'm so sorry.' Vicki
caught her hand.

'Yes, I know.' Jancy pulled her to her feet. 'Come
on, Vicki. Stop crying. You've got to take Duncan
home.'

'But I can't. I can't leave you. Not like this.'

'Yes, you can. I've learned to live with it. It's
Duncan we have to think of now.' And she pulled
Vicki into the hall. 'Here's your coat, put it on quickly.
And your bag. Hurry.'

'What about my things?' Vicki asked in a dazed
voice.

'I'll send them on to you. Here, take Duncan's coat,
his car keys are in the pocket. You can drive his car,
can't you?'

'Yes. Yes, I suppose so. But Jancy, I can't just go
like this.'

'Yes, you can.' Jancy kissed her. 'Look after
Duncan for me. Try and make it up to him.'

Pulling Vicki outside, they found Duncan in the
garden, sitting on the bench seat, his head in his
hands. Still too shaken to protest, he let Jancy bundle
him into the passenger seat of his car, then looked
dazedly round 'Jancy? What are you——?'

But Jancy slammed the door shut and yelled at
Vicki, 'Go on! *Go.* Get him away from here.'

With a sob, Vicki started the car and put her foot
on the accelerator, narrowly missing the fence as she
shot out of the yard. Then she went careering errat-
ically down the lane, dashing tears from her eyes as
she tried to see.

Jancy stood in the middle of the lane &
them go, standing there until the car's head.
no longer visible across the moor. Only then
become aware of her surroundings. A con
tremor ran through her and Jancy began to shive.
controllably. She turned and found Rob standing o.
a couple of yards away. He opened his arms and sh.
went to him, let him hold her as he took her back
inside, avoiding the mutilated portrait in the sitting-
room, into the warmth of the kitchen.

He held her like a child, gently stroking her hair
and murmuring, 'My poor lass. My poor lass.'

Jancy wasn't crying any longer but it was a while
before the trembling stopped. Then she sat up and
pushed her hair back from her face. 'It's OK. I'm all
right now. I won't cry any more. I'm done with
crying.'

'Would you like a drink?'

She shook her head. 'No.'

Their glasses and coffee-cups were still on the table
where they had all been sitting, chatting so casually.
Jancy looked at it and was unable to believe that
everything had changed so quickly. Getting to her feet,
she automatically began to clear the table.

'Why didn't you tell me?' Rob asked from behind
her.

She shrugged. 'I didn't want pity.'

'But you needed someone to talk to. You've been
bottling this up inside. Didn't you tell anyone? Not
even Vicki?'

'No. It was—it was my problem.'

'...u're a young fool,' he said roughly. 'And ...a bigger fool not to tell Duncan. You should ...ven him the chance to——'

'...n't you see his eyes?' Jancy interrupted sharply. '...en he saw my—when he looked at me. He was ...volted by what he saw. I knew he would be. I've ...always known it. That's what I tried to avoid, by running away and coming here. I always knew that look in his eyes would be the hardest thing to bear.'

'Jancy, lass.' Rob came to put his hand on her shoulder, his voice heavy with a sympathy he didn't have the words to express.

'It's OK. Really. In a way, I'm glad that it's out in the open and it's all over. I'm glad they've gone.' She cleared the last of the dishes and smiled at Rob. 'Thank you for lending me your shoulder; you don't know how much I appreciate it. But now I'm going to ask you to go; I'm very tired.'

'You can't expect me to leave you here alone,' he protested.

'You must. Think what the neighbours would say.' And Jancy managed to summon up a laugh. 'Honestly, I'll be all right. I'll be able to sleep now that they've gone.'

Rob continued to protest, but Jancy was firm and there was little he could do. He looked at her intently. 'You won't do anything—you'll promise me you won't hurt yourself,' he said forcefully.

Steadily returning his gaze, Jancy said, 'No. I give you my word I won't.'

He nodded reluctantly, still not completely satisfied, but turned to go. She waved goodbye to him from the front door, then locked and bolted it. But

instead of getting undressed when she went ⬛
room, Jancy changed into thick cord trousers,⬛
and her padded anorak. Knowing that Rob wo⬛
watching, she went downstairs in the dark an⬛
herself out of the back door, slipping through ⬛
garden and over the wall on to the moor.

There was an almost full moon that lit her way
clearly and even cast her shadow across the ground.
The moor was a different, mysterious place at night,
the scent of gorse and heather strong in the air. There
was little noise, just the occasional call of a night-bird
and the pitiful bleat of a lamb that had lost its mother,
instantly cut off when the ewe was found. Striding
steadily along, Jancy didn't stop until she came to the
highest point of the moor. She paused then, looking
around her, and thinking that the moor hadn't
changed in a thousand years, that it must have looked
this way right down through the ages to primitive man.
The moor and the stars.

Sitting down on a rock, she thought how small she
and her troubles were compared to time and space.
Strangely, it was a comforting thought. Her life
stretched ahead of her like an empty road, perhaps
long, perhaps terribly short. But she didn't cry over
it. As she had told Rob, she was done with crying.
And she was glad that Duncan knew the truth, glad
that he was gone. Perhaps he and Vicki would get
together for keeps. For a moment the thought hurt,
but then she was fiercely glad. She loved him so much;
she could only wish for his happiness.

She tried to think positively of the future but could
only think of the past. And the past kept coming back
to that terrible moment when she had seen her own

in Duncan's eyes. Her mind shied away from
and she remembered what Rob had started to
that she hadn't given Duncan a chance. Maybe
had been unfair not to tell him, she mused. But
Duncan was an honourable man, he would have gone
ahead and married her. Though would it have been
out of pity more than love? Would she have had to
watch as he averted his eyes rather than look at her
chest, see him catch himself as he automatically went
to caress her left breast but then remembered, and
awkwardly sought the other? And every time he made
love to her, would she think that he was doing it, not
because he wanted and needed her, but because he
had to convince them both that he was still in love
with her? It was a risk Jancy wasn't prepared to take.

The phrase caught in her mind, making her stop
short and concentrate on it. Going back over the past,
but looking at it from a different angle, she sat for a
long time, thinking it through, seeing everything in a
new light.

The damp rising from the ground formed a low
mist. Feeling cold suddenly, Jancy got stiffly to her
feet, rubbing her gloved hands on her arms to get
warm. It wasn't so easy to see with the mist but it was
a walk she had often taken and was familiar with and
she knew that if she did get lost she had only to keep
going downhill and she would eventually come to the
beck.

But when she was only halfway back she saw lights
in the distance and knew that they came from her
cottage. Rob must have got worried about her and
come back, found her gone. She sighed, hoping he
hadn't roused the village and sent out search parties,

and began to walk faster. Her feet crunch
small stones that lined the track leading do
the moor, echoing loud in the silence of the
'Jancy?' She heard her name called and then
sound of running footsteps. The figure of a m
emerged from the darkness, coming quickly toward
her. It wasn't Rob. It was Duncan.

She stood still, letting him come up to her. He
stopped a few feet away, hesitated for a fraction of a
second, then strode forward and swept her into his
arms.

For several long minutes neither of them spoke, but
then Jancy said in distress, 'Why did you come back?
Oh, why did you come back?'

He put a trembling hand in her hair. 'Did you really
think I wouldn't want you? No matter what happened to you? I love you, Jancy. Nothing can change
that.'

Keeping his arm round her, he led her back to the
house and into the sitting-room. The portrait had
gone, all the pieces picked up and the easel and paints
cleared away.

'Here, sit by the fire.' He pulled up the settee and
put on some more logs, then brought her a drink.
Squatting down, he said, 'I'm just going to tell Vicki
that you're all right. I won't be more than a few
minutes.'

'Where is she?'

'Down at Rob's. He's looking for you, too, but
Vicki will let him know you're safe.'

'I told him I wouldn't do anything crazy.'

w, but we were worried about you.' Leaning
a he brushed her cheek with his lips. 'I won't
ıg.'

ıll right.' But as he went to go, she said,
uncan—come back alone.'

He smiled at her, his eyes warm. 'Of course.'

He was back before she'd taken more than a few
sips of the brandy he'd poured for her; closing the
door, taking off his coat, shutting out the rest of the
world.

'Rob isn't still out there?' she questioned.

'Vicki sounded the car horn; he'll hear it and come
straight back.' Sitting down beside her, he took her
free hand.

She nodded and said, 'I'm sorry to be such a nuisance. I didn't intend to be. I just wanted to get out
in the open and think.' Lifting her head, her eyes wide
and vulnerable, she said, 'You shouldn't have come
back. You should have gone with Vicki.'

He shook his head. 'No way. For a while I was
hardly aware that I was in the car. Seeing you—
realising what you'd been through...' Again he shook
his head as if denying the memory. 'When I realised
what was happening I made Vicki stop. At first she
refused to turn the car round. She said that you would
be too emotional, that I should give you some time
to recover. We had a short, sharp row that only ended
when I lifted her bodily out of the driving-seat and
took over the wheel.'

Jancy gave a wistful smile. 'Caveman stuff, huh?'

Duncan smiled in return. 'Definitely. Finish your
brandy.' She obeyed him and he took the glass from
her, then put his arms round her. 'I shouldn't have

let you push me out of the house,' he said
'But it was such a shock, so unexpected. But r
a shock for me, what must it have been for you
you found out?'

'It was pretty devastating,' Jancy acknowledged

His arms tightened round her. 'I had been imagin
ing everything that was terrible, but never that.'

She sighed. 'I didn't want you to know.'

'Why not? Why didn't you tell me?'

Sitting up straight, Jancy pushed her hair back with
a suddenly tired hand. 'You're an artist, you love
beauty. When we made love you were always telling
me how much you loved my body, how——' her voice
broke for a moment '—how beautiful you found it.
Well, now I'm not beautiful any more, I'm ugly, and
you hate ugliness.'

Jancy had expected every reaction but the one she
got. His face white with anger, Duncan caught her by
the shoulders and swung her round to face him. 'Do
you think so little of my love for you that you could
seriously believe that? If something had happened to
me would you have expected me to walk out on you?'

'No, of course not, but——'

'Then why should you think my love for you so
much less than yours for me? What happened to you
was terrible, Jancy, but you had no right to hide it
from me. Love is for always, whatever happens to
either of us. By running away without telling me, you
turned that love into something small and
unworthy——'

'No,' Jancy broke in. 'I watched your face when
you saw me. You couldn't bear to look at me. You
put up your hand to cover your eyes——'

ldn't bear to think of the hurt you'd been
h,' Duncan interrupted her roughly. 'To think
you'd gone through that alone.' He stood up to
e her. 'All right, I'm not going to deny that it will
ke some getting used to; it must for any man who
suddenly finds that something so terrible has happened to the woman he loves.'

'No, it's hardly something you can overlook,' Jancy
agreed bitterly. Then, seeing his mouth twist in pain,
she reached up to touch his arm and pull him down
beside her again. 'I'm sorry. I know it's been a shock
to you, and I know what you're trying to say.'

His eyes dark and pleading, Duncan said roughly,
'This is what I'm trying to say.' And drew her into
his arms to kiss her.

It awakened all the old fires, that kiss, and for those
wonderful minutes she surrendered to it, never
wanting it to end. When Duncan at last lifted his head
he held her close against him still.

'Now do you understand what I'm saying?' Duncan
demanded, his eyes on her face. Jancy nodded, all
the love she felt for him in her eyes. 'And will you
come home so that we can get married?'

But Jancy sighed and straightened up. 'Please,' she
said, taking his hand. 'Listen to me. There's something else I want to tell you. When I went out on the
moor tonight I thought I was going out there to say
goodbye to you all over again in my heart. But then
I began to think and I realised that I had run away
because *I* couldn't bear you to look at me and because *I* thought you'd find me ugly. I began to see
that it wasn't you I was running away from, but
myself. I hated what I'd become. Until you came I'd

never even looked at myself in the mirror. day you arrived, I wanted to tell you the truth s I wanted to have your comfort and your str Her hands tightened on his. 'I had to make m look in the mirror to remind myself how ugly a deformed I was. It was the only way I could find th strength to resist you.'

'Oh, Jancy, my poor darling.'

'Crazy, mixed-up fool, you mean,' she said on an unsteady note. 'I didn't give you the chance of going on loving me because I no longer had any love for or pride in myself. I'd never thought of myself as a vain person, but it seems that I was, and if I couldn't bear to look at myself then I didn't see how you possibly could either.' Her green eyes awash with unshed tears of sorrow, Jancy said, 'I'm sorry, Duncan. I've been unbearably cruel to you.'

'Yes, you have.' Lifting his hand he gently ran his fingers through her hair. 'But the cruellest part was not letting me share the pain with you, not letting me be there to love and support you.'

Turning her head, Jancy kissed the back of his hand. 'I know. I'm sorry.'

'But at least you've come to understand your own motives. Now we can only go forward and pick up our lives again.'

She nodded, but there was uncertainty in her eyes.

'What is it?' he said sharply.

'What I've discovered about myself; it's all so new. I think I need time to learn how to stop hating myself before I come to you. Otherwise I might start putting the blame on you again, and I don't want that. It will never be as perfect as it was, but——'

be,' Duncan insisted forcefully. 'Basically
no different, you're still the woman I love and
. And it will be much easier to come to terms
n yourself if I'm there to help you.'

She smiled and put her hands on his face as she
kissed him. 'Thank you. But you don't have to be
afraid. I will come—but just let me find the person
I was first.'

'Then let me stay with you.'

But she shook her head.

'If you're thinking that there was anything between
Vicki and me, then you couldn't be more wrong. I
admit I was driven into trying to make you jealous,
but when she came downstairs last night all I did was
try to win her over to my side and make her tell me
what had happened to you. Do please, my darling
Coppernob, do as I ask and come home.'

'No.' She said the word firmly. Looking steadily
into his grey eyes, her hands still on his face, Jancy
went on, 'I want you to go home and wait for me. I
want you to—to tell your family what happened and
ask them to forgive me, for what I did to them and
for what I did to you. I want you to go back to your
job, and start getting the oast-house ready for us. I
don't want you to worry about me any more. And I'll
come very soon. I promise.'

'I don't want to leave you.' The words were torn
from him.

'I know, my darling. But you must give me a little
time.'

'You won't run away again?'

'No.' She smiled and sat back. 'Where would I run
to? You're far too good at finding me.'

Picking up her hands, Duncan looked down a
as he toyed with her fingers. 'All right,' he sig
'I'll do what you want.' His head came up, his ,
thrust forward determinedly in the way she remer
bered and loved. 'But I'm going to set a date for our
wedding and if you're not back in London before then
I'm going to come up here and fetch you.'

Jancy laughed, the first time she had laughed with
real pleasure in months. 'OK, it's a deal.'

'And you'd better wear this.' Getting up, he went
over to his jacket and rummaged in the pocket, came
back and slipped her engagement ring on her finger.

She stared at it, tears in her eyes. 'You had this
with you all along?'

'Of course I damn well had it with me,' he said
huskily. 'Why the hell do you think I came to find
you?' Jancy burst into tears and he pulled her roughly
to him and held her tightly. 'I'm not going yet. I'll
go tomorrow. Now I want to just hold you and feel
you close to me again.'

So they spent the night sitting in front of the fire,
talking sometimes, kissing sometimes, but mostly just
silently grateful to be together again, trying to forget
the past, tentatively groping towards the future.

Duncan left in the morning, taking Vicki with him.
Jancy watched them go, then turned away to try and
find some confidence in herself again.

She tried very hard. Every day she looked at herself
in the mirror, trying to get used to what she had
become. She creamed her legs and did her nails, put
on make-up and messed around with new hairstyles
as she used to. But she had to force herself to do it
all, there was no real interest. She just didn't care

her body any more. Even going into York to round the clothes shops couldn't arouse any nhusiasm. Duncan wrote to her nearly every day and often rang her on Rob's number. At first he didn't push her, but after a couple of weeks she could hear the note of impatience in his voice, and after a month he didn't attempt to hide it any more. 'I've booked the church for a June wedding,' he told her. 'So I want you back here in May latest.'

Conscious that she was failing him as well as herself, Jancy cried out, 'Don't rush me. Don't rush me.'

The time came round for her to go to see the consultant for her usual routine check-up. The waiting-room was crowded with women, as it always was, a lot of them with their husband or a friend, but the majority of them alone. Most of them were middle-aged or elderly, but around them all was an aura of anxiety. 'Will I be all right? Is this lump I feel just a cyst or is it cancer? Will I pass again this time?'

The doctor was running late, as always, the women going in as their names were called. After a long interval one woman came out of the consulting-room in tears, to be met by a friend who put her arms round her in useless comfort. Most people came in almost unnoticed, but then there was a little ripple of interest as the door opened and an elegantly tall, beautifully dressed woman came in. She was comparatively young, only a few years older than Jancy.

The seat next to Jancy was empty and the woman came over to sit beside her. Jancy removed some magazines from the chair and smiled. 'I'm afraid all the appointments are running over an hour late.'

'Not to worry; I've got pienty of time.'

The woman picked up a magazine and read and Jancy went back to hers. But she kep the woman sideways glances, thinking how con she looked. But then she had been just as confr the first time she had been to see a consultant, th had been no one to warn her of the terrible thing tha lay ahead. As Jancy sat there she felt more and more that she just couldn't let this poor woman walk into the consulting-room without a word of encouragement. As it came next to her turn, she impulsively turned to the other girl and said, 'Please. I'm not trying to interfere or anything, but—but if you go in there and the—the prognosis isn't good, please don't be afraid. Having your breast off isn't the end of the world. They're doing it to save you. They——'

'Yes, I know,' the young woman interrupted calmly.

'—only want to...' Jancy stopped, frowning. 'You know?'

'Yes, I had my breast off a couple of years ago.'

Jancy stared at her in disbelief. 'But you can't have. You look so—so confident, and—elegant.'

'Of course.' Jancy's name was called and the girl leaned forward. 'Look, let's go and have a coffee when you come out.'

Bewildered, Jancy nodded.

'Ten out of ten,' the consultant told her, when he'd examined her, and Jancy felt the usual gratitude and relief of tension, a tension that would gradually build again as the weeks passed.

The other woman stood up when she came out. 'My name's Lyn Heath,' she told her. 'There's a coffee shop in the hospital. The coffee isn't very good but at least we can talk.'

they were settled with their coffees at a
⊐, plastic-topped table, Lyn said, 'You've had
breast off, too, haven't you?'

'Yes, last September.'

'And you haven't got over it mentally yet.' Jancy
shook her head wordlessly. 'Are you married?' She
looked at Jancy's hands.

'No, I'm engaged.' She looked down at Duncan's
ring on her finger and suddenly found herself telling
this stranger about being a model, about running
away, everything.

'OK, so you were a model,' Lyn said. 'So why aren't
you modelling now? And why don't you get married?'

'How can I possibly?'

The other girl laughed. 'What on earth is stopping
you? My partner certainly doesn't mind.'

'Your partner? Oh, I see what you mean. He came
to terms with—with the operation?'

'He wasn't around when it happened; I met him
since. And he wasn't the first one. The way I see it,'
Lyn went on, 'they're darn lucky to get me. My one
breast is as good as anyone else's two any day. And
as for modelling clothes—do I, or you, look as if we've
only one breast? Of course we don't. No one can tell.
When I lost my breast I made up my mind it wasn't
going to make any difference, and that's what you
must do, too. Why sit hunched up and wear those
grotty old clothes? You must go on being proud of
your body, not ashamed of it. And don't hate
yourself; cancer isn't a punishment, it's a curable
illness. You wouldn't go around like that if you'd had
pneumonia or something, would you? So why for
this?'

'It isn't the same,' Jancy protested, but th.
a smile in her eyes.

'No, it isn't,' Lyn agreed. She gave a rich la
'But a mastectomy is like marriage—there is life a.
it!' But then she leaned forward and said earnest,
'I know the risks as well as you do. But I made up
my mind that if I was going to die then I was going
to make darn sure that I enjoyed every minute of every
day that I've got left. It's the only way, Jancy. You've
got to pick up your life and control it, not be con-
trolled by fear of what might never happen. And the
chances are on our side; every day they're making new
breakthroughs in cancer research.'

Jancy nodded, her eyes very bright. 'Yes, I know—
and thanks,' she said huskily.

Lyn drained her cup and stood up. 'I'd better go
back to the waiting-room. I'm glad we met. Will I see
you here when you come for your next check-up?'

Getting to her feet, Jancy shook her head firmly.
'No, I'm going back to London. I'm going home.'

It was a few days later when the phone rang in
Duncan's office late in the afternoon. Alone, he picked
it up, his attention still on the drawing in front of
him. 'Duncan Lyle.'

'Well, hello, Duncan Lyle. Would you happen to
be free tonight?'

'Jancy!' He dropped the pen he was holding and
sat back, his mouth widening into a smile of happiness that lit his face. 'Where are you?'

'Just answer the question.'

'Yes, of course I'm free. I'm free for the rest of
my life.'

chuckled. 'Good, it may take that long.'

r what?'

er voice became tender. 'To show you just how
uch I love you.'

He gave a groan deep in his throat. 'Jancy, where
are you?'

'In London. I've borrowed Vicki's flat. She's gone
away on an assignment for a few days.'

'I'll be right round.'

'No,' she said quickly. 'Why don't you look out of
your window?'

'What?' He got up quickly and looked out. Jancy
waved to him from the phone box across the street
where she was standing. The old Jancy, standing tall,
and fashionably dressed, life and vitality in her eyes.

'Well, what are you waiting for?'

He was beside her in less than two minutes, running
across the road to sweep her into his arms and kiss
her in frustrated hunger. When he let her go he held
her at arm's length, his eyes going over her in surprise
and pleasure. 'You look fantastic! What happened to
you?'

She laughed. 'I met a guardian angel.'

'Well, I'm certainly glad you did. It worked a
miracle.' He tucked her arm in his. 'Where to?'

'To Vicki's place, of course.' She smiled into his
eyes. 'We have a lot of catching up to do.'

'We have, indeed.'

But when they reached the flat he turned to her and
said, 'You're sure? About this? About marriage?'

She nodded, her eyes bright. 'Yes, if you are.'

'I've always been sure.'

He reached out to take her hand to lead
the bedroom, but Jancy paused and said, 'Yo
it can recur?'

'Yes. I've been reading it up.'

'The odds aren't that good.'

He drew her into his arms. 'We'll make them good
Together we can beat it. My darling. My precious
love.'

Cruel Legac

One man's untime
death deprives a wife o
her husband, robs a
man of his job and
offers someone else the
chance of a lifetime...

Suicide — the only way
out for Andrew Ryecart,
facing crippling debt. An
end to his troubles, but
for those he leaves
behind the problems
are just beginning, as
the repercussions of this
most desperate of acts
reach out and touch the
lives of six different
people — changing
them forever.

**Special large-format
paperback edition**

**OCTOBER
£8.99**

W●RLDWIDE

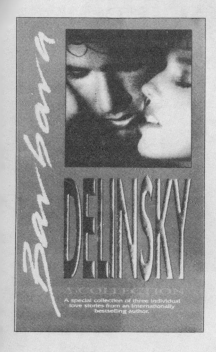

NORA ROBERTS

SWEET REVENGE

Adrianne's glittering lifestyle was the perfect foil for her extraordinary talents — no one knew her as *The Shadow*, the most notorious jewel thief of the decade. She had a secret ambition to carry out the ultimate heist — one that would even an old and bitter score. But she would need all her stealth and cunning to pull it off, with Philip Chamberlain, Interpol's toughest and smartest cop, hot on her trail. His only mistake was to fall under Adrianne's seductive spell.

AVAILABLE NOW   **PRICE £4.99**

W●RLDWIDE

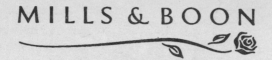